"My Things,"
"All M

She swayed like a reed in the wind, her eyes becoming unfocused. "They're all . . . they're . . . all . . ."

Jackson closed the distance between them in one swift stride, catching the redhead as she pitched forward in a faint. He slipped an arm behind her knees and picked her up, cradling her against his chest.

He was assailed by an almost primitive sense of recognition. He shifted the woman slightly, adjusting his hold on her. Her head lolled against his shoulder. A few stray strands of her flame-colored hair tickled the underside of his jaw.

A surge of protectiveness welled up within him. And something else besides. Something deeper, darker and infinitely more dangerous.

Dear Reader,

It's hard for me to believe that summer is almost over and autumn is right around the corner. For those of us who live where it gets cold, that means we have to start pulling out our sweaters and bundling up our bodies. (If you live where it's warm all year-round, well, we'll just envy you the good weather!) And if you have kids, it's time for them to go off to school, probably providing you with some wonderful quiet time!

During that quiet time I hope you'll pick up more than one of this month's terrific Silhouette Desire romances. We have some special treats in store for you! First, there's the start of a new miniseries from Ann Major called SOMETHING WILD. Its first book, *Wild Honey* is the *Man of the Month*. Next, we have *another* wonderful series, BIG BAD WOLFE, from the talented pen of Joan Hohl. The first book here is *Wolfe Waiting*.

The month is completed with four more romantic, sensuous, compelling love stories. Raye Morgan brings us her unique brand of magic in *Caution: Charm at Work;* Carole Buck heats up the pages with *Sparks;* Anne Marie Winston creates something very wonderful and unusual in *Chance at a Lifetime;* and Caroline Cross makes a sparkling debut with *Dangerous*.

So take time off *for yourself*—you deserve the break—and curl up with a Silhouette Desire!

All the Best,

Lucia Macro
Senior Editor

CAROLE BUCK
SPARKS

SILHOUETTE *Desire*®
Published by Silhouette Books New York
America's Publisher of Contemporary Romance

SILHOUETTE BOOKS
300 East 42nd St., New York, N.Y. 10017

SPARKS

ISBN: 0-373-05808-X

First Silhouette Books printing September 1993

All the characters in this book have no existence outside the
imagination of the author and have no relation whatsoever to
anyone bearing the same name or names. They are not even
distantly inspired by any individual known or unknown to the
author, and all incidents are pure invention.

Printed in the U.S.A.

CAROLE BUCK

is a television news writer and movie reviewer who lives in Atlanta. She is single. Her hobbies include cake decorating, ballet and traveling. She collects frogs, but does not kiss them. Carole says she's in love with life; she hopes the books she writes reflect this.

To the brave men and women
who face down hell
for a living.

Special thanks to
Station 10.

One

Lieutenant Jackson Stuart Miller was hot and bothered.

Neither condition was new to him. Jackson was a firefighter with fourteen years' worth of experience under his helmet. Being hot and bothered went with the job.

It was also something of a family tradition. There'd been Miller men fighting fires in and around Atlanta, Georgia, ever since Jackson's great-great-granddaddy had volunteered for the force back in 1870.

At the moment, Jackson was hot because it was a sizzling June evening and he'd spent the previous hour battling a blaze that had generated a hellish amount of heat. He'd done this while toting more than forty pounds of turnout gear—a knee-length coat, protective pants, gloves, boots and a helmet—plus another forty-five pounds or so of breathing apparatus. There wasn't an antiperspirant in the world that was capable of staunching the flow of sweat from his laboring body.

And there was no quick cure-all for his bothered state of mind, either. The building he and his colleagues had fought so hard to save had been lost. Jackson took such losses very personally. He always had. He figured he always would.

That no one had been injured or killed in this particular fire was something for which he was profoundly thankful, of course. Still, he knew that pieces of people's lives had been destroyed by the blaze. Never mind that the majority of the victims probably had insurance up to their eyebrows. Jackson understood there were some things that couldn't be priced . . . or replaced.

The fire had gutted most of a small apartment house, which catered to childless, white-collar professionals with a taste for high ceilings, elegant moldings and hardwood floors. Jackson's station had answered the second alarm on the blaze. The call had been the fourth of their around-the-clock shift. It had come in right as they'd been sitting down to an already long-delayed supper.

The fire—in the parlance of the profession—had been "well involved" by the time they'd pulled up to it. In other words, a good portion of the three-story frame structure had been burning.

As the ranking officer for his station's "A-shift" truck squad, Jackson had followed mandated procedures and reported to the captain who was in charge of the scene. The initial deployment orders had been aggressive—masks on, ladders up, lines stretched into the building and nozzles opened right into the face of the flames.

The smoke had seemed as thick as a shroud when Jackson had gone in. There'd been embers dropping all over the place. He'd instinctively played turtle, hunching his shoulders up, pulling his head in. His personal fear meter had been running in the red.

Jackson's father had died twenty years earlier, while fighting a fire in a frame building. Captain Nathan Miller had been working the nozzle on a water-charged one-and-a-half-inch hose when the structure had kicked out without warning and come crashing down on top of him. He'd never had a chance.

Jackson realized there were a lot of ways for a firefighter to get hurt or killed. Heck, he'd taken a load of buckshot in the backside four years ago while battling a seemingly "simple" blaze in a small house! Still, being trapped by a collapse was his private nightmare. So when he'd felt a wood brand bounce off his back not thirty seconds after he'd gotten into the apartment house, his adrenal gland had gone into overdrive.

Jackson knew there'd been a time when he would have despised himself for feeling afraid. Fortunately he'd learned a lot in the years since he'd been a gung-ho probie. And one of the most important lessons he'd mastered was that fear— like a hook, a ladder or a hose line—could be an invaluable tool in fighting a fire. It was possible to be scared *smart*... and being smart usually saved more lives and preserved more property than being brave and brainless.

Eventually the offensive approach ordered by the captain had become too dangerous. The fire had pushed, and pushed hard. Jackson and everyone else had had to retreat. They'd backed out of the building and knocked down the fire from the outside. "Surround and drown" was the slightly sardonic designation for this strategy.

Jackson took a deep swallow from the container of water he was holding and eyed the ruined apartment house. While nightfall was approaching, the gray-violet light of dusk did little to soften the ugliness the fire had left behind.

A camera crew from one of the local television stations was taking shots of the smoldering structure. Jackson wondered fleetingly how much coverage this story would get on the 11 p.m. news. Twenty seconds, perhaps? Maybe thirty, if there wasn't much else happening?

The TV crew would almost certainly be gone from the scene before the fire department was. As Jackson well knew, the department's job didn't end just because the flames were out. Once everybody caught his or her breath and gulped down enough liquid to replace at least some of the fluid he or she had sweated off, the site had to be overhauled—that is, checked for hot spots and other hazards. At the same time, basic information about the people who'd been burned out of their apartments had to be gathered. In addition, a determination about the cause of the fire had to be made. If the cause couldn't be determined or was deemed to be suspicious, the arson squad had to be notified.

And wrapping up and returning to the station wouldn't mean it was time to kick back and take it easy, either. Every piece of equipment had to be inspected and restored to prime operating condition. Once that had been squared away, there *might* be an opportunity to indulge in a little "downtime."

Then again, there might also be another fire alarm to be responded to. Or a 911 emergency call involving anything from a twenty-vehicle collision to a kitten up a tree to be handled.

Jackson drank from the container again, then offered it to a black firefighter named Ralph "Fridge" Randall who was standing to his right. Massively built and impressively mustachioed, Fridge was part of Jackson's truck crew. The possessor of a rafter-shaking, soul-stirring bass voice, he sang gospel every Sunday—in church if he was off duty, around the station if he was not. He also wielded an ax more effectively than anyone Jackson had ever seen.

"Thanks, man," Fridge said as he accepted the container. He proceeded to drain it in one long guzzle.

"Maybe we should find you a nozzle to suck on," Jackson kidded. At six foot one and one hundred and ninety hard-muscled pounds, he was accustomed to being the big man in a lot of crowds. Nonetheless, he tended to feel a tad overshadowed when he stood next to Fridge. Except in burning buildings. When he ended up next to Ralph Randall inside a burning building—something which happened a lot, since they frequently buddied up during victim searches—the only thing he felt was damned glad to have such a good firefighter by his side. Jackson quite literally trusted Fridge with his life.

"Forget the suckin'." Fridge made a dismissive gesture with the emptied water container. "You find me a nice, tender hose, I'll start *chewin'*."

"Hungry?"

"Let's just say my belly button may start rubbin' up against my backbone any minute. You think our shift's *ever* gonna get to sit down, say grace and have a decent supper again?''

Jackson tipped his helmet back and dragged the back of one hand across his forehead. He was conscious of a certain emptiness in his own stomach. ''Maybe sometime after Labor Day.''

''This is—what? The fifth time in a row we been nailed?''

''Sounds about right.''

Fridge heaved a sigh. ''At least *this* one was a workin' fire. I mean, workin' fires is why I joined the department. I lose a meal to one, I don't mind. It's the garbage runs that are startin' to get to me, you know? Smoke scares. False alarms. Things like that diddly squat stove fire we caught last Saturday night. Man, somebody could've spit on that and put it out. And the stink! I tell you, Jackson, it took me two whole days to get the smell of whatever that woman was cookin' cleared out of my nose. You ask me, her family was lucky she burned up their dinner. The whole bunch of 'em probably would've ended up with some dire form of food poisonin' if she hadn't.''

''And we probably would've gotten the 911 call.''

''Too true.'' Fridge grimaced. ''And some of us probably would've gotten puked on in the process. Speakin' of which—you hear about the 911 call B-shift caught, day before yesterday?''

''You mean the one with the naked drunk who was seeing little green men and big pink elephants?''

''Yeah, that's it. Only I think the men were pink and the elephants were green.'' The black firefighter shook his head. ''Man, 911 is supposed to be for *emergencies*. The public keeps gettin' us jacked up over nothin', we won't have the energy for the real stuff.''

''Well, somebody's got to do—''

Jackson broke off abruptly, an odd sense of awareness shivering through his nervous system. A split second later, he heard a voice. It was soft and shaky and seemed to come from a few feet to his left.

''N-no,'' the voice said. ''Oh . . . dear Lord . . . *no*.''

Stiffening, Jackson pivoted. As he did, he could have sworn he caught the scent of flowers. Ninety-nine times out of a hundred, the only thing he could smell in the immediate aftermath of a fire was smoke. Yet all of a sudden, his nostrils were twitching in response to the faint but unmistakable fragrance of flowers.

The source of the shattered-sounding denial was a tall, willowy redhead who appeared to be in her early thirties. Her delicately drawn features were taut. Her skin was as white as chalk. She was staring at the wreckage of the apartment house, her expression full of anguish.

Jackson had seen such looks of loss before. For one sickening moment, he was afraid that he and the others had done something far worse than failed to save the building.

Oh, God, he thought, his gut knotting. There was somebody in the place. Somebody no one knew about. Somebody we didn't get out.

He could only imagine who that "somebody" might have been to the redhead. A relative? A friend? A...lover?

The woman lifted her hands—ringless, trembling—and pressed them to the base of her slender throat. She shook her head back and forth, her lips working soundlessly.

Jackson reached out slowly, not wanting to spook the redhead. His first on-the-job injury had come from a woman whose husband had been killed in a high-rise fire. She'd become hysterical when she'd realized what had happened and attempted to run into the still-burning building. He'd restrained her. She'd flailed at him with her fists, knocking his helmet off and smacking him square in the face. His nose had been broken as a result of the blow.

"Ma'am?" he questioned softly, pitching his voice to soothe.

No response. The redhead just kept staring at the apartment house and shaking her head. She seemed to be in shock.

"Ma'am?" Jackson repeated, his tone a trifle more insistent. "Do you live here?" He took a cautious step toward the woman. Glancing out of the corner of his eye, he saw that Fridge had backed off a bit. He understood the rea-

son. The unfortunate reality was that a lot of people were
unnerved—intimidated, even—by Ralph Randall's size and
skin color when they first encountered him.

After a moment, the redhead shifted her gaze away from
the smoldering shell of the apartment house. Jackson experienced a strange jolt of emotion when she finally made
eye contact with him. He'd never felt anything like it. Not
even the first time he'd met the sassy blond coed who'd become his wife and given birth to his only child.

He was gripped by a sudden, visceral sense that he knew
this red-haired woman. Really, truly *knew* her. Which was
impossible. How could he "know" a woman he was willing to swear on a Bible he'd never laid eyes on before in his
life?

"Ma'am?" he questioned once again, conscious that his
voice had thickened and his pulse accelerated. While the
dimness of twilight and the dilation of the redhead's pupils
made it impossible for him to ascertain what color her eyes
were, he was ready to bet on green. A deep, cool green, with
maybe a spark of gold.

The woman's pale, elegantly shaped hands fluttered like
wounded doves. She swallowed convulsively, then ran her
tongue over her lips. "Was...was anyone hurt?" she asked,
staring up at him.

Jackson shook his head. "No, ma'am. Not as far as we
know. Looks like everybody got out all right."

"Oh." She nodded. "G-good." She nodded again. After
a moment, she shifted her gaze away from Jackson's face
and back to the ruined apartment building.

"Ma'am—"

"My things," she whispered. "All my things." She
swayed like a reed in a wind, her eyes becoming unfocused.
"They're all...they're...all..."

Jackson closed the distance between them in one swift
stride, catching the redhead as she pitched forward in a
faint. He slipped an arm behind her knees and picked her
up, cradling her against his chest.

Again, the subtle scent of flowers teased his nostrils.
Again, he was assailed by an almost primitive sense of rec-

ognition. He shifted the woman slightly, adjusting his hold
on her. Her head lolled against his shoulder. A few stray
strands of her flame-colored hair tickled the underside of his
jaw. A surge of protectiveness welled up within him. And
something else besides. Something deeper, darker and infinitely more dangerous.

Jackson was a skeptic when it came to things like predestination. Still, he couldn't escape the feeling that the woman
he was holding in his arms was meant to be—

"Hey, man, you okay?"

Jackson glanced from the redhead's fair-skinned face to
Fridge's dark one. The look in his friend's eyes—a little
puzzled, a lot perturbed—made him uncomfortable.

"Yeah," he responded tersely, struggling to control his
expression. As close as he was to Fridge, what he was feeling right now was private. Very... very private. "I'm just
fine."

He was lying, of course. He wasn't just fine. He wasn't
anywhere near okay, either.

What Lieutenant Jackson Stuart Miller was, was hot and
bothered. The kind of hot and bothered that had nothing to
do with being a firefighter.

The air circulating in the car was cool.

The music issuing from the vehicle's tape deck was calm.

The driver savoring both was Dr. Phoebe Irene Donovan, the newest member of the psychiatric staff of one of
Atlanta's largest hospitals. She was heading home after a
very long day at work.

While the job Phoebe had started just two months ago
was proving even more satisfying than she'd dared to hope
it would be, it was also turning out to be extremely stress-
ful. Her patient load was heavy. Her paperwork burden,
even worse. To say that the responsibilities of her new position "weighed down" on her at times was to understate the
case.

And then there was pressure of trying to earn the accep-
tance of her new co-workers. Phoebe realized that she was
still on probation with most of them. She was being judged

professionally... and personally... at all times, in all situations. Everything from her intellectual integrity to her appearance was being scrutinized.

Exactly how long this situation would continue, she couldn't begin to predict. Although Phoebe sensed her performance to date had won her a fair amount of respect, she was well aware that her age and sex—even her status as a transplanted Yankee—were working against her to a certain degree. If she'd been a forty-three-year-old born-and-bred Georgian male with a wife and two children instead of a thirty-four-year-old single female from Boston, she probably would have had little or no trouble finding her niche in the staff hierarchy.

Of course, the evaluation process wasn't one-sided. Phoebe had spent the past eight weeks assessing her new colleagues just as carefully as they'd been assessing her. And with a few exceptions—the kinds of exceptions that flourished in *every* institutional setting—she'd been impressed by what she'd observed.

The traffic light Phoebe was approaching went from green to yellow. She eased her foot down on the brake, bringing her car to a halt as yellow changed to red. Vivaldi gave way to Bach on the tape deck.

"Thank God, it's Friday," she murmured, contemplating the weekend ahead. Her schedule was blissfully blank. The final item on her four-page "settling in" list had been crossed off that morning. There was nothing to prevent her from playing couch potato for the next two days.

Nothing, that is, except her own nature.

"Do you ever relax?" Alan Brinkley, the man she'd seen buried on what was supposed to have been their wedding day, had asked her shortly after they'd first met.

"Not really," she'd answered. *"It makes me ... tense."*

Phoebe smiled wryly, remembering how Alan, who'd been granted a tenured professorship at Harvard at the academically tender age of thirty, had laughed about that response. It had become something of a running joke between them. She hadn't minded the teasing, though, because Alan had made his admiration of her drive and discipline clear from the beginning of their relationship. Only one man in her life had ever applauded her achievements more enthusiastically. That man had been her father, Dr. Lyle Donovan.

Phoebe felt her smile fade. An all-too-familiar sense of sadness settled over her.

Lyle Donovan and Alan Brinkley.

Her father and her fiancé.

Both gone....

Phoebe sighed and closed her eyes for a moment. She was aware that a number of the friends and colleagues she'd left behind in Boston were convinced her decision to move to Atlanta had been a form of running away from her past. That they'd arrived at such a conclusion was understandable. There was no denying that Boston held many painful memories for her. It had, after all, been the setting for the most wrenching moments of her life.

Yet Phoebe honestly believed she'd come to terms with those moments. She'd embraced them. Absorbed them. Accepted how they'd shaped who and what she was. In her mind, coming to Atlanta was part of the positive process of growing up and moving on. She regarded her new job as a meaningful opportunity, not an avenue of escape.

The honk of a horn made Phoebe open her eyes. The traffic light had changed from red to green. She shifted her foot from the brake pedal to the gas. The car surged forward.

Steering her thoughts back to the weekend ahead, Phoebe debated what she should do between now and Monday. Getting acquainted with Atlanta seemed the most sensible option. Her knowledge of the city was extremely limited. Yes, she'd ferreted out the necessities—a well-stocked supermarket, a dependable dry cleaner, a browsable bookstore and so forth. But beyond that...

Well, beyond that, she was still at the point where she had trouble remembering the difference between Peachtree Street and Peachtree Road. And she was darned if she was *ever* going to be able to keep Peachtree Parkway, Peachtree

Terrace and Peachtree Industrial Boulevard straight in her head!

Eventually Phoebe turned onto the tree-lined street where she now lived. She slowed her car, glancing from side to side, watching for children and pets. The last few rays of sunlight were fading fast. Soon, it would be dark.

The street curved sharply to the right about a block before her apartment house. The sight that confronted Phoebe as she rounded the bend caused her to gasp.

Fire trucks.

One. Two. Three of them.

Dear God. It looked as though they were parked directly in front of her building!

She couldn't see the three-story structure itself. It was set back from the street and shielded from view by a group of oak trees. Still, Phoebe knew the worst.

She "knew" it the way she'd known it the night the shrilling of a telephone had awakened her from a dream about the wedding that was supposed to take place just four days later.

She "knew" it the way she'd known it the afternoon she'd watched her father suddenly clutch his chest and collapse on a tennis court.

No, she protested silently. Oh, please, no.

Phoebe pulled over to the side of the street, killed the car's engine and set the emergency brake. After undoing her seat belt—no easy task, given the unsteadiness of her fingers—she opened the car door and climbed out.

"Oh, God," she whispered as she got her first real look at what was left of the place she'd been calling home since the end of April. Her stomach churned as she took in the devastation. Bile rose in her throat and flooded her tongue. For a moment, she thought she was going to be sick.

And then nausea gave way to an awful kind of numbness. Phoebe started forward.

She had to find out what had happened. She had to make some kind of sense of what she was seeing.

There were two helmeted and heavily garbed firefighters standing together just up ahead of her. One was white. He was tall and broad-shouldered. The other was black. He was just plain huge. Something about the two men communicated the message that they were bonded by friendship as well as a common profession. Phoebe headed for them.

She stumbled to a halt a few feet away from the pair. The closer she got to the apartment house, the worse it looked. She'd left a structure of gracious solidity that morning. She'd returned to little more than a gutted shell.

"N-no," Phoebe said on a shuddery exhalation. "Oh... dear Lord...*no.*"

It was denial. Obviously. Inevitably. Phoebe had seen the reaction in too many patients not to recognize it in herself. But that didn't stop her from trying to repudiate reality.

She'd lost the two people she held nearest and dearest before she'd come to Atlanta. And now...

Her father's books. The small but select collection of first editions that had seemed to capture the loving and learned essence of the man who'd raised her. Destroyed.

Alan's photographs and letters. The tangible evidence of their mutual caring and commitment. Gone up in smoke.

She had nothing left! *Nothing!*

"Ma'am?"

The inquiry was soft. Insinuating. It came from one of the firefighters and it was tinged with southern-style gallantry.

Phoebe didn't respond. She just kept staring at the smoldering ruin in front of her and shaking her head.

"Ma'am?" It was the same male voice. This time, however, there was a hint of demand in the Dixie drawl. "Do you live here?"

It seemed like a cruel question to Phoebe. How in the world could she *live* here? No one could possibly—

Oh, God. The others. What about the other tenants?

Phoebe shifted her gaze from burned-out building to the firefighter standing nearest her. She tilted her head back.

"Ma'am?" the firefighter repeated. His voice sounded different. Husky. Almost hoarse. He seemed...disturbed.

Phoebe made a vaguely defensive gesture with her hands. She swallowed hard, several times, then licked her lips. She couldn't think straight. Something was happening to her. Something that went beyond the shock of the fire.

"Was . . . was anyone hurt?" she finally asked.

The firefighter shook his head. "No, ma'am. Not as far as we know. Looks like everybody got out all right."

"Oh." She nodded. "G-good." She nodded again. She couldn't seem to stop. Her breathing pattern was unraveling. Her heart was pounding.

Phoebe's gaze slid away from the firefighter, back toward the ruined apartment building. She wanted to weep.

"Ma'am?" The question seemed to come from a great distance away.

"My things," she whispered. "All my things." The world began to blur and spin. Phoebe tried to stabilize herself, but her bones had turned to jelly. "They're all . . . they're . . . all . . ."

"All" became nothing as Dr. Phoebe Irene Donovan fainted for the first time in her life.

Two

"**C**ongratulations!" an ebullient male voice announced. "You've reached 555-2378. I'm unavailable at the moment. But don't despair. If you can answer the following three questions correctly, you'll win a personal telephone call from me!"

Phoebe almost slammed down the phone. Was *everybody* in Atlanta "unavailable" on this particular Friday afternoon? she wondered. Not one of the calls she'd placed during the past fifteen minutes had connected her with a human being!

"Okay," the voice continued cheerfully. "Here goes. Question one—What is your name? Question two—What do you want? Question three—What is your phone number? Wait for the beep, or you'll be disqualified. Good luck!"

Phoebe massaged her temples. She really wasn't in the mood to talk to another answering machine. Particularly not one with a cutesy recorded request for a message.

Still, she had to admit that the Apartment for Rent ad which had prompted her to call 555-2378 seemed promising. She was determined that she was going to find a new place to live this weekend. Seven days in a motel was more than enough.

Beep!

"This is Dr. Phoebe Donovan," she said. She was beginning to feel like one of Pavlov's famous dogs. Except instead of salivating at the ring of a bell, she'd been conditioned to spit out her name and number at the sound of a beep. "I'm calling about the apartment you advertised in the newspaper. I'd like to come by and see it tomorrow—that's Saturday—or the day after, if possible. I don't have a permanent telephone number just now, so I'll try you again. Thank you very much."

Phoebe dropped the receiver back into its cradle and consulted her wristwatch. The final item on her work week schedule—a group therapy session involving about a dozen adolescents with substance abuse problems—was scheduled to begin in twenty minutes. She decided she could squeeze in one more call.

She scanned the classified section of the *Atlanta Constitution* she had spread out on her desk, winnowing through the listings she'd hurriedly circled when she'd picked up the newspaper that morning.

A "cozy condo" near Emory University. Hmm...

"Cozy" could be a real-estate euphemism for "cramped." Still, the price was absolutely right. And the neighborhood, according to several of her co-workers, was very pleasant.

Phoebe paused for a moment, contemplating the support she'd received from her colleagues during the past week. She'd been deeply touched by their expressions of sympathy and offers of assistance.

She certainly hadn't expected the "rally 'round" response she'd gotten. As a matter of fact, she hadn't even intended to inform anyone at the hospital about what had happened to her. Her insurance agent, however, had had other ideas. He'd tried to contact her at her office shortly before she'd arrived for work Monday morning and, in the course of leaving a message, had uttered the words "fire" and "losses." The person who'd taken the message had quickly spread the bad news. As a result, she'd been confronted by a barrage of concerned questions the moment she'd come on duty.

Although her answers to those well-meaning questions had been truthful, they hadn't been complete. For reasons Phoebe hadn't been able to sort out to her own satisfaction, she'd remained silent about both her unprecedented fainting spell and the firefighter who'd caught her when she'd crumpled like a rag doll.

At least, she *assumed* he'd caught her. When she'd come to, she'd found herself propped up against the running board of one of the fire engines. A freckle-faced paramedic who hadn't appeared old enough to qualify as an Eagle Scout had been fussing over her. Neither the broad-shouldered firefighter nor his jumbo-size buddy had been anywhere in sight.

She could have asked the paramedic about her apparent rescuer, of course. But she hadn't. An emotion she still couldn't—or wouldn't—identify had caused her to hold back from doing so. And she'd been equally reluctant to pursue the matter with the clipboard-toting firefighter who'd interviewed her about the fire and the property loss she'd sustained because of it.

Phoebe sighed. She should have found out the man's name, she told herself for the millionth time. What's more, once she'd found it out, she should have used it to track the man down so she could thank him for the consideration he'd shown her!

So why hadn't she?

Good question. One worthy of examination by Sigmund Freud himself.

To begin with, she'd been upset. Terribly upset. And some instinct had told her that the firefighter in question—for all his soothing southern drawl and courtly manner—wasn't likely to do much to restore her peace of mind.

Beyond that . . .

Oh, all right. Beyond that, she'd been embarrassed by her passing out and the weakness it had seemed to imply. She was a doctor, for heaven's sake. An honors graduate of one of the most demanding medical training programs in the country. She'd been exposed to operating theaters and emergency rooms. She wasn't supposed to swoon like the virginal heroine of some Victorian melodrama!

Phoebe shook her head. Enough of the self-analysis, she decided firmly. Suffice to say, she'd been under a tremendous amount of stress the previous Friday and her handling of it had been less than exemplary. There was nothing she could do to change that. She had to put the episode behind her and move on.

As for the matter of her anonymous Galahad in fireproof gear...well, chances were that theirs had been a once-in-a-lifetime encounter. And even if their paths *did* happen to cross again, she probably wouldn't recognize him. Because she hadn't really seen the man.

Noticed that he was tall, tanned and apparently well built? Yes.

Been conscious that he exuded an aura of masculine assurance? Sure.

But "seen" him in the sense of being able to describe him in detail or summon his image in her mind's eye? No. *Definitely not!*

Sighing for a second time, Phoebe turned her attention back to the classified ads. All right. She wanted something in the immediate "metro" area. No long commutes for her. Nothing too big. Nothing too new. And nothing that smacked of a swinging singles complex, either.

She suddenly focused on a listing for an apartment described as being "airy, well kept" and "close to Inman Park." She knew a bit about the neighborhood. As a matter of fact, she'd come close to renting a place there when she'd first moved to Atlanta.

Airy.

She liked the sound of that. Assuming it didn't mean there was a hole in the roof, of course.

Well kept.

That was an appealing adjective, too. It seemed to imply a certain pride of property. And it was a lot more believable than the word "immaculate," which seemed to appear in every third listing.

Phoebe picked up the phone and dialed the number at the end of the Inman Park ad. Maybe this time she'd get lucky. Maybe this time she'd get to speak to a person instead of a soulless hunk of technology.

The click of connection.

One ring. Two rings. Three—

"Hello?"

The voice was soft and sweet. It was more mature than a child's, but not quite a woman's. Braced as she was for a recorded message, Phoebe didn't respond to it right away.

"Hello?" the voice repeated with a tinge of impatience. "Tommy John Purdy, if this is you again—"

Phoebe cleared her throat. "Hello," she said calmly. "My name is Donovan. Dr. Phoebe Donovan."

"Oh." An embarrassed giggle bubbled through the line. "I'm so sorry. It's just that there's this boy in my school— Tommy John Purdy. He thinks he's in love with me or somethin' and he keeps callin' up to hear the sound of my voice sayin' hello. He never says anythin' back, though. Which is pretty rude, if you ask me. 'Course, it could be worse. He *could* be breathin' like some sex maniac on the other end of the line. That's what Keith Lowell did to Betsy Carter a few months ago. But now they're goin' steady, so I guess you could say it turned out all right. Still, if Tommy John breathed on me, I'd probably have to tell my daddy. And Lord only knows what he'd do. See, he—my daddy, that is—has been actin' kind of weird ever since I started goin' through puberty. It worries me sometimes. 'Specially since I have my sweet sixteen next year. I *think* he's goin' to be okay with me gettin' my driver's permit. But when I start datin'..."

Phoebe had bitten down on her lower lip about halfway through this artlessly engaging recitation. She knew that laughter—even appreciative, empathetic laughter—would be misinterpreted. Adolescent angst, no matter how amusingly expressed, had to be treated with respect.

"A lot of fathers find it difficult when their daughters start to mature," she commented after a moment, shifting into the neutral tone she often employed during therapy sessions. "They have trouble accepting the fact that their dependent little girl is growing into an independent woman."

There was a brief silence, then the girl echoed Phoebe's last three words. "'An independent woman,'" she said, uttering the phrase as though it were a badge of honor. "That's what I want to be."

Inexplicably touched, Phoebe said, "I'll bet, deep down, that's what your father wants you to be, too."

"Oh, I *know* he does," came the unequivocal response. "Daddy truly respects people who stand on their own two feet. He's always tellin' me, 'Lauralee Miller, you can be anything you want to be, if you just set your mind to it.' And he means it."

Phoebe believed her. She decided that whatever anxieties "Lauralee Miller's" father might have about his daughter's maturation process, he sounded like a sensitive and supportive parent.

"That's a wonderful attitude, Lauralee," she observed. "My father used to tell me something very similar when I was growing up."

"Really?"

Phoebe smiled, remembering. "Yes. Really."

"Wow. What did you want to be?"

The question caught Phoebe off guard. "Ah, well, I, ah—"

"Oh, Lord," the girl exclaimed, plainly distressed. "You must think I'm just awful. I mean, you probably called here for some very important reason. But before you got a chance to say anythin', I started pourin' out my private problems and pryin' into your personal life. And we haven't even been introduced! I'm Lauralee Miller. Only you probably figured that out, right? Now, I know you told me your name, but I don't really remember—"

"Donovan," Phoebe supplied, recovering her poise. "Phoebe Donovan."

"Didn't you say *Doctor* before?"

Phoebe hesitated, feeling oddly reluctant to confirm her professional status. "Yes, I did," she said after a second or two. "I'm a psychiatrist."

"Oh-oh."

Phoebe grimaced, hearing the sudden uneasiness in the girl's voice. "Now, don't get uptight, Lauralee," she ordered briskly. "And *don't* start picking over all the things you've said during the past few minutes and wondering whether I thought they sounded crazy."

Lauralee gasped. "How did you—?"

"Because it happens all the time."

"You mean, people get…nervous…when they find out what you do?"

"A lot of them, yes."

"That must be hard."

"It can be."

"Well, I'm truly sorry. You just took me by surprise."

"That's all right. I understand."

There was a brief pause. Then, with a hint of humor, Lauralee inquired, "*Did* what I said sound crazy?"

Phoebe chuckled. "No, Lauralee. It didn't sound crazy. It sounded remarkably normal."

"Even the part about my daddy?"

"Actually that sounded pretty special. I'd say you and your father have a very good relationship."

"Yes, ma'am. We're really close." The affection in the girl's voice was palpable. "I guess he worries extra because it's just him and me."

"Probably," Phoebe agreed, squashing the urge to ask what had happened to Lauralee's mother. She waited a beat, then diverted the course of the conversation. "To get to the reason I phoned. There was an ad in the classified section of the—"

"You mean you're callin' about the apartment?"

"Yes. That's right."

"*Great!* It's part of our house, you know. Daddy converted it after—well, because we didn't need such a big place."

"I . . . see."

"It's really nice" came the quick assurance. "You'd have your own entrance and everythin'."

"That's good to hear." Phoebe put a premium on privacy. "I take it the apartment's still available?"

"It sure is. Would you like to come and look at it?"

Phoebe debated with herself. She wasn't too keen on the "part-of-our-house" description. Still, she liked the Inman Park neighborhood. And the rent was reasonable. She really ought to check the place out.

"Yes, I would," she said. "Would tomorrow morning, say between ten and noon, be convenient?" She couldn't be more specific about the time. She had an early-morning consultation with a colleague and she couldn't be certain how long it would last.

"That'd be just fine."

"Are you sure? Maybe your father—"

"He's in the shower right now. But I know tomorrow would be dandy with him."

"All right. About the address—"

"No problem." Lauralee recited the necessary information, then asked, "Do you know where that is?"

"No, not really," Phoebe admitted as she jotted down the street and number she'd just been given.

"Where will you be comin' from?"

"Ah—" Phoebe paused to think "—downtown."

"All right, then. First, you get on Peachtree. Now, you're going to be goin'—"

"Street or Road?" Phoebe interrupted.

"What?"

"Peachtree Street or Peachtree Road?"

"Oh." Lauralee seemed to require a moment to digest the implications of Phoebe's question. "Peachtree *Street.* First, you get on Peachtree Street . . ."

By the time the girl finished delivering her directions, Phoebe felt as though she'd been given a block-by-block tour of the entire Inman Park area.

"Thank you, Lauralee," she said, glancing at her wristwatch. She definitely had to get off the line and get back to work.

"You're welcome, Dr. Donovan. Now, you be sure to call if you get lost, all right?"

"Absolutely," Phoebe promised. "I'll see you tomorrow morning."

"We'll be lookin' for you. Bye."

"Bye."

Jackson Miller's pride and joy was hanging up the telephone as he ambled into his large, cream-and-yellow kitchen, toweling his hair. He'd spent all morning and most of the afternoon doing yard work. A steaming hot shower and a change of clothes had transformed him from sweat hog to civilized human being. Next on his agenda was a long, cold drink.

"Hey, sugar," he said, resisting the urge to ask his daughter to whom she'd been speaking. If the call concerned him, Lauralee would say something. If it didn't...

If it didn't, she'd probably keep it to herself and he'd drive himself nuts with worry. But he wasn't going to pry. No matter how great the temptation, he was *not* going to pry.

He wondered fleetingly if Tommy John Purdy had finally screwed up the courage to open his mouth and respond to one of Lauralee's hellos. He wasn't supposed to know about young Purdy's peculiar form of courtship, of course. He'd discovered what was going on several weeks ago, when he'd answered the telephone in his bedroom a split second after his daughter had picked up the phone in the kitchen. His first reaction, a combination of irritation and amusement, had quickly given way to admiration for Lauralee's handling of the situation and something close to pity for her erstwhile swain's shyness.

"Oh, hi, Daddy," Lauralee replied, turning around. There was a sparkle of excitement in her big, blue eyes. She was smiling. The braces on her teeth glinted in the sunlight streaming in through the kitchen windows. "Guess what?"

Games. Oh, Lord. She wanted to play games. Playing games had been fine when it had meant peekaboo, hide-and-seek, or Go Fish. But now?

"What?" Jackson returned, slinging the towel he'd been using on his hair around his neck. He padded over to the refrigerator and yanked it open. He'd intended to have some iced tea. But maybe he'd do better with a beer.

"The person I just got through talkin' to on the phone?"

Jackson bent down, pushing aside a pitcher of lemonade, a carton of milk and a head of lettuce. "Yeah?"

"Well, it was somebody who might be interested in rentin' the apartment."

Jackson breathed a brief prayer of thanks, then chastised himself for getting all worked up over nothing. If he kept on like this, he was going to be dead of stress before Lauralee reached the age of consent.

The age of consent.

Oh, God. He didn't even want to think about it!

There didn't appear to be any beer in the refrigerator. Feeling a bit desperate, Jackson grabbed hold of a can of diet soda. He straightened and turned back toward his daughter. "A prospective tenant, hmm?"

Lauralee nodded, her short blond curls dancing around her heart-shaped face. "Uh-huh. Her name is Donovan."

Jackson bobbled the aluminum can, nearly dropping it. No, he thought. No. It can't be.

The willowy redhead. The one who smelled like flowers and who had fainted into his arms. *Her* name was Donovan. Dr. Phoebe Donovan. She was a newcomer to Atlanta and she was a psychiatrist on the staff of one of the city's major hospitals.

Jackson knew all this because he'd tracked down the man who'd collected the resident information after the apartment house fire and questioned him about the red-haired woman. That his action had been less than professional, he was willing to concede. But he'd had to ask. He'd been so damned *haunted* by her memory and the response she'd stirred in him that he'd had to find out who she was.

"Daddy?" Lauralee prompted, an odd note in her voice.

"Sorry, sugar," Jackson said automatically. He popped the tab on the soda. "You say the lady's name is . . . Donovan?"

"That's right. Phoebe Donovan. She's a psychiatrist."

Jackson raised the can to his lips and chugged down about a quarter of its artificially sweetened contents. It was a wonder he didn't choke on the stuff.

"She asked if she could come over tomorrow between ten and noon and look at the place," Lauralee continued. "I said that was fine." She paused, furrowing her brow. "That *is* okay, isn't it, Daddy?"

Jackson gestured with the soda can. "Couldn't be better, Lauralee."

Seeing Dr. Phoebe Donovan again was just what he needed, he decided abruptly. Because there was no way another meeting with her could generate the reaction he thought he'd experienced during their first encounter. That initial reaction had been some kind of...of...well, he didn't know what it had been. But he was ready to lay odds that it had been the result of dehydration and adrenaline more than anything else.

So, fine. He'd see the lady for a second time. He'd shake her lily-white hand and say, "How do you do?" Then he'd show her around. If she decided she wanted to rent from him, terrific. If not, no skin off his backside.

"She seemed *really* nice," Lauralee commented. "I wonder what she looks like."

"A redhead," Jackson responded, then wished he could recall the assertion. For reasons he couldn't adequately explain, he preferred his daughter not know about his previous contact with Phoebe Donovan. At least, not yet. If the good doctor should happen to remember him—which, given how distraught she'd been, he seriously doubted she would—he'd deal with the matter then.

Lauralee wrinkled her nose. "No, I don't think so, Daddy."

It took Jackson a moment to realize that his daughter had assumed he was guessing about Phoebe Donovan's appearance. "You don't?"

"Nope. She didn't *sound* like a redhead."

"And just how does a redhead sound, sugar?"

"I don't know, exactly. But not like Dr. Donovan. I think she's a brunette. With short hair, like mine, only more sophisticated."

Jackson shook his head. "Long red hair."

His daughter eyed him for several seconds. "Want to bet?"

"Depends on the stakes."

"If you're right, I bake you a peach pie," Lauralee proposed. "If I'm right, you do the dishes for a week."

"Wash and dry?"

"And put away."

Jackson raised the soda can to his lips and drank, pretending to contemplate the matter. "Okay. Done," he said after a few moments.

Lauralee flashed a mouthful of wired teeth, clearly confident of victory. Then she asked, "What about Dr. Donovan's eyes?"

"I'd be willing to lay money she has two of them."

"Daddy!" Lauralee giggled. "I meant what about the *color* of them."

"Oh. And here I thought I had a sure thing. The color of Dr. Donovan's eyes. Ahh…green. Green, with maybe a few flecks of gold."

"No *way*," his daughter scoffed. "Brown. Definitely brown."

"You want to make another bet?" Jackson challenged. He didn't intend to hold his daughter to their wager, of course. But it was fun teasing her.

The older she got, the less he seemed able to do that. There'd been a time when communication between them had been free and easy. No more. Lauralee was going through a touchy stage of life, so he'd learned to weigh every word, consider every quip, before uttering it. For all her resilience—and Jackson knew his only child was as strong and smart as she was sweet—Lauralee's feelings could be as bruisable as orchid blossoms.

"Two peach pies against two weeks of doin' dishes?"

"You're on."

There was a pause. Eventually Lauralee asked, "What if Dr. Donovan turns out to be a blue-eyed blonde?"

Jackson finished the diet soda and crushed the can with one hand. "Then all bets are off."

Three

Phoebe pulled up in front of the Miller house shortly before eleven the following morning. She was halfway in love with the place by the time she'd gotten out of her car.

The house was a graceful, two-story structure. It was painted white with a few whimsical touches of gingerbread trim picked out in blue. Its meticulously tended lawn was punctuated by a number of stately shade trees. The trees—their leaves rustling in a gentle June breeze—were ringed with beds of brightly blooming flowers. A similar show of blossoms flanked the driveway.

Sitting in the driveway was a red pickup truck. It was being hosed down by a tawny-haired man Phoebe assumed must be Lauralee Miller's father. Her reaction to him was a lot more complicated than her reaction to the house.

The man washing the pickup was tall. An inch or so over six feet. He had broad shoulders. A sleekly muscled back. Long, powerful-looking legs. If he was carrying a superfluous ounce of fat, it didn't show.

He was tanned. It was the kind of tan that looked as
though it had been earned during the course of hard, outdoor labor, not acquired in leisurely increments at the beach.

He was wearing a low-riding pair of wash-faded denim
cutoffs. Nothing else.

He was standing with his back to the street, whistling
melodiously as he sprayed the truck. He seemed oblivious
to Phoebe's approach. As she came to within five or six feet
of him, he bent forward, directing the stream of water from
the hose at the underside of the vehicle.

While Dr. Phoebe Irene Donovan wasn't going to pretend that she was immune to the impact of a good-looking
man, she prided herself on appreciating members of the
opposite sex more for their intellectual gifts than their ana-
tomical endowments. Still, when she saw the way those ab-
breviated denims went from snug-fitting to skintight...

Maybe she made some sort of sound, alerting the tall,
tanned stranger to her presence. Maybe the wind shifted and
he caught the scent of her perfume. Then again, maybe
she was ogling him so obviously he could sense her scrutiny. Whatever the case, the sandy-haired man suddenly
straightened up and turned around, narrowly missing
spritzing her with the hose. A pity, in a way. She probably
could have benefited from a cold shower.

Phoebe discovered she'd been wrong in her assumption
that he was wearing nothing but the cutoffs. He had on a
pair of mirror-lensed, wire-framed sunglasses as well.

"Sorry," the man apologized, deftly twisting the nozzle
on the hose and shutting off the stream of water.

"No harm done," Phoebe answered, controlling an urge
to pat at her hair or fuss with her clothes. That she should
feel this urge nettled her. She understood what her desire to
primp implied.

*Psychology 101. Members of one sex preen for members
of the other to signal attraction.*

She waited for a few moments, expecting the sandy-haired
man to say something. He didn't. He simply stood there,
looking at her. At least she assumed he was looking at her.

Given the impenetrable barrier of his sunglasses, she couldn't be sure.

Phoebe lifted her chin. "Mr. Miller?" she finally ventured. There was something unnerving about this man. Something that went beyond his blatant masculinity. He seemed familiar to her. Yet she was virtually certain she'd never encountered him before.

"Yes, ma'am," he replied. His voice was low, but had the resonance of authority. Phoebe wondered briefly if he might have served in the military. He definitely had a capable-of-command air about him. "And you're—"

"Dr. Donovan?" an eager young voice suddenly called.

Starting at the sound of her name, Phoebe turned toward the Miller house. Coming out of the front door was a blond-haired girl in blue jeans and a powder pink T-shirt. She was petite, no more than an inch over five feet tall, and very pretty in a pixieish way. She exuded the kind of all-American, cute-as-a-button appeal Phoebe would have given just about anything to possess during her painfully awkward adolescence.

"Dr. Donovan?" the girl repeated as she came to a halt a few feet from where Phoebe was standing.

Phoebe nodded, conscious that the girl seemed to be scrutinizing her with unusual intensity. "And you must be Lauralee."

"Yes, ma'am" came the cheerful confirmation. Lauralee smiled briefly, showing off a set of wire-banded teeth. Then she slanted a look at her father and commented with a kind of good-humored resignation, "Guess you'll be expectin' peach pie for dessert tonight...huh, Daddy?"

Puzzled by this apparent non sequitur, Phoebe glanced at the girl's father for some kind of clarification. He wasn't offering any.

"We'll talk about that later, sugar," he told his daughter. "Right now, why don't you show Dr. Donovan around the apartment? I'll finish here, get cleaned up and meet you inside." He returned his attention to Phoebe and asked, "Does that suit you, ma'am?"

"That's fine, Mr. Miller," Phoebe concurred quietly. She was still curious about the "peach pie" comment. She had the strangest feeling that it had something to do with her.

Lauralee's daddy suddenly smiled. The smile revealed several things. Among them, that there were deeply grooved dimples on either side of his sensual mouth and a small chip in one of his top front teeth. The dimples suited him, adding a touch of boyishness to his lean—almost craggy—features. The chipped tooth seemed to go with the faintly crooked line of his nose.

She'd never seen that smile before, Phoebe decided abruptly. She definitely would have remembered it if she had!

"Jackson," he corrected. "Just call me Jackson."

The interior of the Miller house appealed to Phoebe even more than the exterior. The apartment didn't simply live up to the adjectives in the classified ad. It surpassed them.

"Do you like it?" Lauralee asked with disarming directness after she'd finished showing Phoebe around the premises.

"Very much," Phoebe replied truthfully.

"The kitchen's not too small for you?"

"I'm not much of a cook." In point of fact, she was a culinary incompetent. Alan had once teasingly told her that the only thing she should ever make for dinner was reservations.

"Oh." Lauralee sounded slightly surprised. "Well... you're probably too busy to cook much, what with your career and all."

Phoebe made a neutral sound, surveyed the polished wooden floor and freshly painted walls of the apartment's elegantly proportioned living room. She experienced a pang of regret for the furniture she'd lost in the fire. It would have fit so perfectly in this place!

"I sure wish there was more closet space," the teenager said with a sigh, returning to a subject she'd raised several times already. While she'd detailed the apartment's good points with great enthusiasm, she'd been equally quick to describe what she considered its flaws. The comparative dearth of storage space seemed to rank near the top of her What's Wrong list.

"That's not really a problem," Phoebe answered. Even before the fire, her wardrobe had been a pared-down affair. And now...

"I hope you don't mind that squeaky part in the hallway. Daddy says there's no way to fix it, short of tearin' up the place. We've got the same trouble on our side."

Phoebe shook off her momentary lapse into melancholy. What was gone, was gone, she told herself. There was no way to get it back. "I hardly noticed it," she said, giving Lauralee a quick smile. "I grew up in a house that was full of squeaky floors and doors."

"Was that up north?" Curiosity appeared to be as much a part of the teenager's personality as candor.

"Yes. In Boston."

"Is your family still there?"

Phoebe's throat seemed to close up. She swallowed, hard. "I don't really have any family, Lauralee."

"You...don't?"

"No. I'm an only child. My parents are dead. Neither one of them had any siblings. So—" Phoebe gestured "—no family."

There was both shock and sorrow in Lauralee's blue eyes. "That's awful," she said. "You didn't lose both of them at the same time, did you? Your mama and daddy, I mean."

"My mother was killed when I was eighteen. In a car accident." Phoebe saw no reason to add that her mother had been as good as dead to her for many years before that fatal crash. Irene Archer Donovan had abandoned her husband and only child the same week Phoebe had started school. She'd never returned. News of her untimely death had reached Boston purely by chance. "My father died four years ago, of a heart attack."

Lauralee remained silent for nearly thirty seconds. "My mama died when I was seven," she said finally. There was a tiny catch in her voice as she spoke the last word, as though she had to force it out of her throat. "She had cancer."

"I'm sorry, Lauralee."

"Thank you." The girl nibbled on her lower lip, clearly debating with herself. Then she confided, "For a long time, I thought it was my fault. That I must have done somethin' bad, you know?"

"Oh, yes," Phoebe responded softly. "I know. Believe me, I know."

"Then I got really m-mad at her. For dyin', I mean. For... leavin' me and Daddy."

"It's normal to feel that way," Phoebe assured her. Dear Lord, when she thought of the fury she'd directed at her father's memory! And at Alan's. The grief she'd experienced after their deaths had tapped into a wellspring of rage she'd never known existed within her. She'd come to terms with that rage in time, of course. But while it had lasted...

Never again, she thought. Never again was she going to leave herself vulnerable to that kind of hurt. To that kind of anger. The toll such emotions exacted was too high.

Lauralee nodded, her blond curls bobbing around her forehead. "I finally told Daddy," she said. "About bein' mad at Mama. And he said it was okay. He said he felt mad at her, too, sometimes. He said we would work it out together. Bein' mad and sad and everythin' else. And I guess we pretty much did." The girl smiled crookedly, her eyes very bright. "Daddy and me do all right."

Phoebe returned the smile. "I'll bet the two of you do a lot better than that."

"So," Jackson began about five minutes later. He handed Phoebe a condensation-fogged glass of iced tea. "Any questions I can answer for you?"

Phoebe took a drink of the fresh-brewed beverage and glanced around the Millers' sunshine-filled kitchen. Did she have any questions? she asked herself.

Yes. She had a question. But it wasn't one she was about to voice anytime soon.

What was it about Jackson Miller that made her so wary of him?

She liked the man's home. She liked it a great deal.

She liked the man's daughter even more.

But as for the man himself...

Jackson had donned a white cotton T-shirt since their initial encounter in the driveway. While the lightweight garment did little to disguise the power of his upper torso, it did make him seem a bit more... more... well, *civilized* wasn't exactly the word she was searching for, but it was close.

He'd also removed his sunglasses. His eyes were blue. Blazingly, brilliantly blue, with a fine network of lines radiating from their outer corners. His eyes contrasted vividly with his sun-bronzed skin. They also gave away almost nothing of what was going on behind them.

"No, I don't think so," Phoebe replied, setting the iced tea glass down on the small wooden table at which she was seated. Jackson had taken the chair across from her. She looked at him. He was leaning back in his seat, watching her intently from beneath half-lowered lids. "Lauralee told me everything I need to know."

"She wants to rent the apartment, Daddy," the teenager declared in a satisfied tone. She was perched on top of one of the kitchen counters, sipping a soft drink and swinging her legs.

Jackson cocked a brow. It was impossible to tell whether he was pleased or perturbed by his daughter's statement. "Is that right?"

"Yes," Phoebe affirmed after a tiny hesitation. He knew the effect he was having on her, she suddenly decided. He knew and he wasn't quite certain what to do about it. Because *she* was having an effect on—

"When do you want to move in?" Lauralee asked, derailing Phoebe's runaway train of thought. Phoebe turned in her chair. "Daddy's workin' tomorrow, Wednesday and next Saturday, so those might not be the best days. Especially if you'd like some help with your things." The girl paused, then she glanced at her father. "Daddy, do you think Fridge would be willing to give Dr. Donovan a hand?"

"I think he'd be willing to give her *two* hands if she needed them," Jackson replied. There was an odd edge to the response. Phoebe wondered about the reason for it. Was this "Fridge" person a bone of contention between father and daughter?

Lauralee's next words did little to clarify the situation. "Fridge and Daddy are on the same shift at the station," she explained. "So that means he'd be workin' tomorrow, Wednesday and next Saturday, too. But almost any other day—"

"I appreciate your wanting to help, Lauralee," Phoebe interrupted gently. "But the truth is, I've only got a few things to move. I'm going to be starting from scratch when it comes to furniture and all the rest."

"You are?" The girl was clearly taken aback.

Out of the corner of her eye, Phoebe saw Lauralee's father straighten up in his chair. "Yes," she affirmed. "You see, the reason I need a new apartment is that there was a fire in the building where I was living. I lost just about everything."

"Why, that's *terrible!*" Lauralee declared with great emotion. "When did this happen?"

"A week ago last Friday."

"Here in Atlanta?"

Not really expecting it to mean anything, Phoebe supplied the address of her previous residence. To her surprise, Lauralee gave a gasp of recognition.

"I saw that fire on the TV news!" The girl looked at her father, the skin between her brows pleating. "Daddy, didn't you say somethin' about your station answerin' that call?"

Phoebe's gaze slewed toward Jackson Miller. Suddenly everything slotted into place. Suddenly she knew why her prospective landlord seemed so unnervingly familiar.

The firefighter. Dear Lord. Jackson Miller was her there-one-minute-gone-the-next firefighter!

"It was *you*," she said in a voice that sounded nothing like her own. "You were there. You were the one who—"

"Wait a minute," Lauralee cut in. "Daddy—Dr. Donovan—you *knew* each other before today?"

"Not exactly knew." Jackson temporized quickly. "We saw each other—"

"You cheater!" his daughter accused as she exploded. She hopped off the kitchen counter and landed on the linoleum-covered floor with a flat-footed thud. "You *cheater!*"

"Now, sugar—"

"I am *never* bakin' you another peach pie, Daddy! Never. Ever. And when I tell Grammy Miller about your low-down trick, *she'll* never bake you another one, either!"

"I wasn't going to hold you to the bet, Lauralee."

"Hah!" The girl crossed her arms across her chest and stuck her pertly shaped nose into the air.

There was a short, sharp silence. Phoebe's gaze went from Jackson to his daughter. When it became obvious that neither one of them was going to say anything more, she spoke.

"Would someone please tell me what this is all about?" she requested.

Lauralee turned, clearly eager to recount her tale of parental perfidy. "Remember yesterday, when you called?" she began. Phoebe nodded. "Well, afterward, I told Daddy you sounded nice and I wondered what you looked like. He said you had long red hair and green eyes. I said, no, you had short brown hair and brown eyes. And then we made a bet. If Daddy was right, I had to bake him two peach pies— one for your hair, one for your eyes. If I was right, he had to do the dishes for two weeks."

"I . . . see," Phoebe said slowly, not at all certain that she did.

"I *thought* Daddy was guessin' about your colorin', like I was," Lauralee continued in an aggrieved manner. "Only *now* I know he was bein' a total cheater because he'd already seen you!"

Phoebe looked at Jackson. There was one major piece missing from the girl's explanation. "How did you know who I was, Mr. Miller?"

Jackson massaged his nape with the palm of his right hand, obviously uncomfortable. He didn't repeat his suggestion that she call him by his given name.

"Do you remember talking with a firefighter after you regained consciousness?" he inquired.

"Regained consciousness?" Lauralee echoed in a horrified tone. "Dr. Donovan, were you hurt?"

"I just fainted, Lauralee," Phoebe clarified. "I didn't arrive at the apartment house until after the fire was out. I was terribly upset by what I saw and I... fainted. Your father caught me. At least—" her gaze collided with Jackson's "—I *assume* he caught me."

"I did," Jackson confirmed tersely. "But to get back to your original question. Do you remember—"

"Yes, I remember talking to a firefighter after I regained consciousness," Phoebe replied impatiently. "He told me he needed some information for the official—" She broke off abruptly as comprehension clouted her squarely between the eyes. "You got my name from him!"

A nod. "I called him a few days later."

"But, *why?*"

Jackson hesitated, an odd expression flickering across his lean face.

"I wanted to make certain you were all right," he finally replied.

"You could have waited and seen for yourself," Phoebe pointed out. Strange. She hadn't realized until this very instant how much she'd resented his apparent desertion of her.

"No—" a definite shake of the head "—I couldn't have. We got a 911 call from a couple blocks away barely a minute after you passed out. We had to respond. So, I handed you over to one of the paramedics."

Phoebe moistened her lips, feeling inexplicably embarrassed. "I didn't realize."

Jackson held her eyes with his for a few moments, then turned his attention back to his daughter. Shifting her own gaze, Phoebe noted that the teenager had abandoned her indignant, nose-in-the-air stance.

"I apologize for tricking you, Lauralee," Jackson said quietly. "I hope you'll forgive me."

The girl regarded him silently for several seconds then declared, "It was a tacky thing to do, Daddy."

"Absolutely," Jackson agreed. "What can I say? I'm a weak man when it comes to your peach pies."

Lauralee rolled her eyes, but Phoebe could tell she was pleased by the compliment.

"Hey, it's true, sugar."

The corners of the girl's mouth started to curl. "Well..."

"What do you say I do the dishes for the next two weeks as a forfeit?"

"The next *three* weeks."

Jackson cocked a brow. "You're out for blood, huh?"

"Yes, sir."

Jackson let a few seconds tick by, then acquiesced. "Okay. Deal."

His daughter's lips parted in a big braces-flashing smile.

There was another silence, much more pleasant than the previous one. Although Phoebe was reluctant to break it, there was something she had to know. "Mr. Miller?"

Jackson looked at her, his expression wary. "Yes, ma'am?"

"Why didn't you tell me who you were out in the driveway?"

A shrug. The muscles of Jackson's broad shoulders rippled smoothly beneath the stretchy fabric of his T-shirt. "You didn't seem to recognize me. I decided there wasn't much point in raking up what happened."

"I might have wanted to thank you for what you did."

"What I did was part of my job, ma'am."

The statement—utterly simple, profoundly proud—seemed to hang in the air. Then the reality of it came smashing down on Phoebe like an iron fist.

What I did was part of my job, ma'am.

Jackson Miller's "job" was fighting fires. His was the most hazardous profession in the world, according to an article on work-related stress she'd read not too long ago. He saved lives at the risk of his own. He raced into burning buildings while other right-minded individuals were running out of them.

A person could get hurt doing Jackson Miller's job.

A person could get *killed....*

An emotion she couldn't name sliced through Phoebe like a knife. She drew a shuddery breath, struggling for control.

"I wish you wouldn't keep calling me ma'am, Mr. Miller," she snapped.

"And I wish you wouldn't keep calling me Mr. Miller, Dr. Donovan" came the quick retort.

That brought Phoebe up short. She stared into Jackson's sky-colored eyes for several moments. She began to feel a little light-headed. Somewhere in the back of her brain, a voice told her she was on the verge of making a terrible mistake.

Finally she said, "My name is Phoebe, Jackson."

Four

It was shortly after seven-thirty on a beautiful Sunday morning. Jackson Miller had arrived home a few minutes ago. He'd taken his time about getting out of his pickup truck. The reason for his dallying was now jogging up the driveway.

"'Morning, Phoebe," he said.

"Hi, Jackson" came the slightly breathless response. Phoebe halted a few feet away from him. Her cheeks were becomingly flushed, her forehead pearled with perspiration. There was a vivid sparkle in her wide-set green eyes. With her flame-colored hair scraped back into a ponytail, she looked more like a graduate student than a board-certified M.D.

"I didn't realize you ran." His ignorance was hardly surprising, given that his new tenant had been living under his roof—so to speak—for less than forty-eight hours. Jackson had no doubt that what he didn't know about Dr. Phoebe Donovan would fill a book. A very long and complicated book. The kind that probably would include footnotes, a fifty-page bibliography plus a cross-referenced index.

"I got hooked on it in med school." Phoebe wiped her brow with the back of her right hand. The movement caused her small breasts to stir provocatively beneath the sweat-dampened T-shirt she had on. "It's how I unwind and try to stay in shape."

Jackson nodded his understanding, willing himself not to drop his gaze. He'd gotten an eyeful of Phoebe's "shape" a short time ago, when he'd passed her in his truck. He'd turned onto the street where he lived and—*whammo*—there she'd been.

He'd known Phoebe had an attractive figure, of course. How could he not? He'd carried her in his arms. A man couldn't carry a woman in his arms without getting a pretty accurate, uh, *feel* for the way she was put together. Even so, he'd been jolted right down to his socks when he'd come around the corner and caught sight of her. The way she'd filled out those snug white shorts...

"You have a nice stride," he commented abruptly. It was the truth. She ran with a seamless blend of disciplined energy and inbred grace. He couldn't help speculating about whether she might bring the same combination of qualities to other physical activities.

Phoebe's eyes widened but she didn't immediately reply. Jackson had the impression she was taking his remark apart and testing it for hidden meanings. He supposed this response could be a natural by-product of her professional training. Then again, it might very well be the result of her picking up on the fact that he felt like an itchy, twitchy, hot and horny teenage boy every time she came within touching distance.

Just *why* he felt this way was something he had yet to figure out. He'd never really been attracted to redheads. And he'd always preferred women who were compact, curvy and cuddly to those who were lean, leggy and decidedly intellectual.

"Thank you," Phoebe said after a moment, apparently acquitting him of uttering a double entendre. He was tempted to tell her that if he ever decided to act on the desires she aroused in him—something he considered highly unlikely for a whole laundry list of reasons—he'd bypass innuendo and opt for the direct approach. "Do you run?"

"I was varsity cross-country in college." He saw an expression he couldn't quite identify flicker across her fine-boned face. Was it surprise? he wondered. Surprise that he'd gone to college? The possibility annoyed him. He didn't like the notion of anybody—including multi-degreed lady doctors from up north—trying to stick him into some blue-collar pigeonhole. "I usually put in a couple of miles on the days I'm not working."

"You're just coming off work now, aren't you?"

"That's right." The Atlanta Fire Department operated on a rotation shift system. Firefighters were scheduled for twenty-four hours on duty, forty-eight hours off. He wasn't due to report in again until 7:00 a.m. on Tuesday.

"Was it busy?"

Jackson shrugged. "Pretty quiet, actually. Especially for a Saturday."

"You sound disappointed."

And *she* suddenly sounded odd. Almost disapproving. Given the circumstances of their first encounter, Jackson recognized it probably was inevitable that Phoebe would have a certain ambivalence about what he did for a living. But even so...

"A little," he conceded honestly. While he wasn't about to wish misfortune on anyone, he hated slow shifts. "If I spend too much time sitting around the station, I start to feel useless."

She lifted her brows. "Even with six citations for heroism to your credit?"

"How did you—" Jackson began, then broke off as he realized what the only possible answer to his unfinished question could be. "Lauralee."

Phoebe nodded. "She stopped by late yesterday afternoon. She said she was going to spend the night at your mother's house and she wanted to see how I was settling in before she left."

Jackson expelled a breath. He decided he needed to have a little talk with his daughter. "Let me guess. She ended up bending your ear off."

"Well . . ." Phoebe seemed amused, not irritated.

"She's not supposed to be pestering you."

"Oh, she wasn't" came the quick response. "She had some very good ideas about how I should arrange the furniture I rented. In any case, I enjoy Lauralee's company, Jackson—really."

And then she smiled at him, truly smiled at him, for the very first time.

It was an intensely feminine smile. Feminine, but not the least bit flirtatious. As a red-blooded son of the region that was the home of the eyelash-batting belle, Jackson was familiar with flirtatiousness in all its forms. He couldn't see a trace of it in Phoebe's expression. Nonetheless, the curve of her rosy lips seemed to hint at secrets inaccessible to the male of the species. That made him a little edgy.

He suddenly found himself flashing back to high school. He remembered swaggering by small groups of girls, playing it oh-so-cool and indifferent. He remembered the way a lot of those girls had glanced at him, then looked at each other and giggled.

Of course, Dr. Phoebe Donovan wasn't a giggling schoolgirl. Exactly what she was, Jackson was still a long way from determining.

Maybe it was time he started working on the puzzle.

"Join me for breakfast?" he suggested impulsively.

She seemed surprised by the invitation. This was understandable. He was a little surprised by it, too.

"I, ah—" she gestured at herself "—I couldn't."

"I didn't mean right this second," he temporized. Now that the idea was out, he didn't intend to let her reject it. "Take whatever time you need to shower and change, then come over."

Phoebe hesitated, much the way she'd done before she'd used his given name for the first time.

"I'm a good cook, Phoebe."

His comment triggered a rueful laugh. "I'm glad one of us is."

Jackson waited a beat, sensing the situation was tipping in his favor. Then he pressed his proposal. "So? Will you have breakfast with me?"

Another hesitation. He could tell to the instant when Phoebe made up her mind. She squared her slim shoulders and lifted her chin a notch. A moment later she said, "Yes, I will."

Jackson opened his front door before Phoebe had a chance to knock on it.

"That was quick," he said, gesturing for her to enter. His gaze flowed over her like water.

Phoebe stepped over the threshold, resisting a sudden urge to smooth her freshly brushed hair and straighten the casual outfit she'd changed into after showering. She hadn't had much choice about what to put on. Although she'd replaced the working wardrobe she'd lost in the fire, she hadn't gotten around to stocking up on leisure wear.

"I didn't want to keep you waiting," she replied, noting that he'd traded the dark blue uniform he'd been wearing for a loose-fitting Atlanta Olympics T-shirt and a thigh-hugging pair of jeans.

Jackson cocked a brow. "I thought keeping men waiting was one of the things the good Lord put women on earth to do."

For a split second, Phoebe believed the man was serious. Then she saw the roguish glint in his vivid blue eyes and realized she was being teased. An odd jitter of pleasure ran through her.

"Do you say things like that to Lauralee?" she parried.

Jackson grinned, his teeth flashing white against his tanned skin. "And have her turn me in to the National Organization for Women? Or, even worse, tell my mama? No, ma'am. No way, no how."

Phoebe laughed. "I think I'd like to meet your mother," she commented, remembering some of the things Lauralee had mentioned about her Grammy Miller the previous afternoon.

Jackson's expression turned thoughtful. His gaze moved over her once again. Phoebe found herself wondering exactly what he saw when he looked at her. While there was nothing suggestive in the stroke of his sky-colored eyes, it made her acutely aware of her femininity.

"I think she'd be interested in meeting you, too," he said after a moment.

There was a pause. As a student of human relationships, Phoebe knew there was a great deal to be learned from pauses in conversations. She did not, however, feel inclined to analyze the implications of this particular one. After a few increasingly uncomfortable seconds of silence, she sniffed the air and said, "Mmm. Something smells delicious."

Jackson's grin returned. The set of his neck and shoulders relaxed. "Biscuits," he informed her succinctly, then nodded toward the back of the house. "Come on into the kitchen."

To reach the kitchen, they had to pass through a long hallway. The hallway's cream-colored walls were hung with black-and-white photographs. One of them caught Phoebe's eye and she stopped to examine it more closely. It showed a burly man with a bushy mustache standing in front of a horse-drawn fire engine.

"Stuart Nathan Miller," Jackson said. His voice held the same tone of pride she'd heard eight days ago when he'd responded to her statement that she might have liked to thank him for what he'd done for her during their first encounter. "My great-great-granddaddy."

"He was a firefighter, too?"

"Volunteer."

Phoebe studied the picture for several seconds then slanted an assessing look at Jackson. She thought she saw a faint resemblance. "When was this taken?"

"A couple of years after the end of the War Between the States." Jackson's mouth quirked. "That's the conflict you Yankees mistakenly refer to as the Civil War."

"We Yankees won, remember?" Phoebe riposted sweetly. "We can refer to it any way we want."

"Not around a lot of my relatives, you can't."

They both laughed. Then blue eyes met green ones and the laughter stopped. For a moment, Phoebe forgot to breathe.

Jackson was the one to break the eye contact. Turning his attention back to the hallway wall, he gestured to another photograph. "That's my great-granddaddy."

Exhaling sharply, Phoebe picked up his cue and looked at the picture. "He was a volunteer firefighter, too?"

"Yes, ma'am. And that—" he indicated a third photograph "—was my grandfather's station. It's gone now. He retired as a battalion chief."

"Quite a family tradition," Phoebe murmured. She shifted her gaze to the next photograph.

This one showed a man in full firefighter's gear. He was staring straight into the camera lens and smiling. The resemblance to Jackson was striking.

"Your father?" She glanced sideward.

A nod. "Lieutenant Nathan Miller. He was killed in a fire when I was sixteen."

"Lauralee mentioned he'd died in the line of duty."

Jackson stared silently at the photograph of his father for several seconds, then moved on. "That's my mama," he said, pointing to a studio-style portrait of a formidable-looking lady who appeared to be in her mid- to late fifties. Her silver hair was perfectly coiffed, her face flawlessly powdered.

Phoebe tilted her head to one side, assessing the picture. Jackson's mother reminded her of a head nurse she'd worked with during her internship. The woman had been one of the most impressive—and intimidating—medical professionals she'd ever known. Nurse Jenkins had never raised her voice, never seemed to ruffle a hair. Yet senior surgeons had reacted to her the way buck privates reacted to four-star generals.

"I *don't* think I'll mention the Civil War around her," she decided after a few moments.

"Good idea," Jackson replied dryly. "Her great-great-granddaddy on her mama's side rode with General Stonewall Jackson."

"Is that why you're named—?"

"Yes, ma'am."

There was one more photograph on the wall. Unlike the picture of Jackson's mother, it appeared to be a candid shot. It showed a radiantly pretty blonde playing with a fair-haired pixie of a girl. The bond of affection between the two was palpable.

Phoebe felt her throat tighten. "Lauralee's mother?" she asked.

Jackson nodded. "Her name was Anne. With an *e*. She was very particular about that *e*."

His tone was full of tenderness. Yet it also held an undercurrent of humor, as though he was remembering some joke he'd shared with the woman he'd wed. Phoebe suddenly recalled what Lauralee had confided to her about Jackson's admission of anger over his wife's untimely death. It seemed plain to her that he'd come to terms with his anger in a very positive fashion.

"Was Anne from Atlanta?"

"No. Baltimore. Her older brother and I were roommates in college."

"He introduced you?"

Jackson gave a wicked chuckle. "Heck, no. Steve did everything he could to keep his sweet little sister out of my clutches."

"Then how—?"

"Let's just say that the worse Steve told Anne I was, the more interested she got."

"How bad were you?"

"Oh, I did a few things during the course of my college career I'd just as soon my mama never hears about. But nothing I'm truly ashamed of. And I still managed to collect my diploma."

"What did you get your degree in?"

"Engineering, with a minor in business administration."

Phoebe blinked. "From engineering to firefighting?"

"Anne reacted that way, too, at first," Jackson admitted frankly. "We got married right after I graduated and settled here in Atlanta. I had a nice, solid job. Then one day, I ran into an old friend of my father's who mentioned that the fire department was going to start hiring again. There'd been a freeze on because of budget problems and a bunch of court cases. Anyway, this old friend nudged me into applying. I made it through all the tests and was notified to report for recruit training. Anne and I went around and around about whether I should or shouldn't. She even talked with my mama a couple of times. She finally said she knew I'd regret it for the rest of my life if I didn't try, so she told me to go ahead."

"Which you did."

"Which I did." He paused, his gaze straying toward the photograph of his father. "And after fourteen years—"

He broke off as a shrill, buzzing sound erupted from the kitchen.

"Wha—?" Phoebe asked, startled.

Jackson gestured. "Time to have breakfast."

They were still "having breakfast" several hours later when the phone rang. Grimacing at the interruption, Jackson got up to answer the call.

"Hello?" he said into the receiver. "Oh." His voice mellowed. "Good morning, sugar."

Phoebe rose to her feet and began transferring the dishes they'd been using from the kitchen table to the sink. She glanced at her wristwatch as she did so. A jolt of shock went through her as she registered the time.

It was past eleven o'clock!

Was it possible? she asked herself. Was it possible that she and Jackson Miller had spent more than *three hours* talking to each other? She would have guessed that the elapsed time had been no more than, say, maybe thirty minutes. Granted, they'd covered a wide range of topics—disagreeing sharply on a few, discovering they shared views on a surprising number of others—since they'd sat down at the breakfast table.

"Lauralee says hi."

Phoebe started slightly, then looked at Jackson. He'd apparently just hung up the phone. He was smiling.

"Phoebe?" His smile faded and a line appeared between his tawny brows. "Are you all right?"

"Oh, yes." She nodded. "I'm fine. But I just noticed the time. I'm sorry, Jackson. I didn't realize I'd been here so long. It's nearly eleven-thirty."

He crossed to where she was standing. "So?"

"So, I'm sure you have a lot of things to do."

"Not a one," he replied easily, relieving her of the two juice glasses she was holding. His fingers brushed hers as he did so. Although the contact was brief and seemingly accidental, it triggered a tremor of response deep within Phoebe.

If she'd been given to blushing—which, unlike many redheads with milky-fair complexions, she wasn't—Phoebe knew she would have done so then. An unsettling kind of heat licked along the nerve endings just beneath her skin.

She cleared her throat. "Well, actually, *I* have a million errands to run," she said, patting her hair. Her voice was steady. Her hand, a little less than.

"I understand," Jackson responded, setting down the glasses. He studied her silently for a moment then said in a casual tone, "Speaking of running..."

Phoebe got a grip on herself. "Yes?"

"Could you tolerate some company the next time you hit the road?"

Her grip on herself slackened abruptly. "You mean you?"

Jackson nodded, his gaze very direct.

"You want to go running with me?" She cringed inwardly at how inane this question sounded.

"If you wouldn't mind."

"Ah—" she shook her head "—no."

"No?"

"No, I wouldn't mind," Phoebe clarified. Was it her imagination, she wondered, or had the space that separated her and Jackson shrunk considerably during the past few seconds?

"How about tomorrow morning?"

It took Phoebe a moment or two to remember what day of the week tomorrow would be. Jackson's proximity—the man definitely had maneuvered himself closer to her!—was very distracting.

"Tomorrow morning," she repeated. "Monday. Well, um, it'll have to be early. I need to leave for the hospital by eight-thirty."

"No problem. I'm up with the chickens. Say, six? Out front?"

Phoebe nodded. "It's a date."

Her response, she assured herself afterward, had been only a figure of speech.

Lauralee dragged her last French fry through the pool of ketchup she'd poured onto her plate, then lifted it to her lips. "How old were you when you went on your first date, Phoebe?"

Phoebe smiled at the girl who, in the space of just three weeks, had become like the kid sister she'd never had but always secretly wanted. The two of them were lunching at one of the restaurants in Atlanta's largest malls after a long morning of shopping. "I was eighteen."

The French fry landed on the table with a tomato-smeared splat. *"Eighteen?* Were your parents strict, or what?"

Phoebe laughed. Every once in a while, Lauralee's Dixie drawl gave way to the teenybopper diction frequently heard on the television sitcoms. "Or what," she replied. "Nobody asked me out until I got to college."

A frown furrowed Lauralee's forehead. "Was your high school all girls? Like a convent?"

"No. It was coed."

"There must have been something *totally* wrong with the boys you knew, then."

"Let's just say that none of them was anxious to go out with a tall, skinny redhead who walked around with her nose stuck in a book." Phoebe paused, thinking back to the misfit years of her adolescence. She'd been worse than a wallflower by teenage standards. She'd been a weed. Awkward. Insecure. Academically accelerated but socially inadequate.

Lauralee grimaced. "Boys are so immature."

"Well, I wasn't exactly dream-date material and I knew it." Phoebe smiled wryly then admitted, "I would have given just about anything to look like you back then."

The comment was intended as a compliment. But Lauralee's reaction to it was more glum than gracious. Slumping in her chair, she heaved a sigh and said in a dismal voice, "You mean you wanted to be...*cute*."

"Ah, yes, I suppose." Phoebe spent several seconds trying to figure out why the teenager seemed to disdain the adjective so much. "You don't like being cute, Lauralee?"

Another gusty sigh. "I don't want to be ugly," Jackson's daughter conceded, wrinkling her turned-up nose. "It's just that, um, remember the first time we talked on the phone? When you said that thing about growin' up into an independent woman?"

Phoebe nodded.

"Well, I don't think it's possible to be cute and an independent woman at the same time. And I truly aspire to be an independent woman."

A smiled tugged at the corners of Phoebe's lips but she refused to give in to it. She suddenly recalled another fragment of her first conversation with the teenager. "'Lauralee Miller,'" she quoted, "'you can be anything you want to be, if you just set your mind to it.'"

The girl's cornflower-blue eyes widened, then she dimpled and giggled. "You want to hear somethin' sort of funny, Phoebe?" she asked after a few moments.

"Love to." Phoebe caught the eye of a passing waiter and signaled for their check.

"You said you used to want to look like me, right? Well, if I ever get over bein' cute, I want to look like *you*. You're elegant."

"Why, thank you, Lauralee."

"You're welcome. I wouldn't mind bein' a little exotic, either. Like Keezia Carew, maybe."

Because many of her patients were teenagers, Phoebe made a conscious effort to remain au courant when it came to who was hot and who was not on the teen culture scene. Yet she came up blank when she tried to match the name Lauralee had just mentioned with a face from a music video, movie or TV show.

"Who?" she finally queried.

"Keezia Carew. She works with Daddy."

Phoebe experienced an unfamiliar and rather unpleasant twist of emotion. "She's a firefighter?"

Lauralee nodded, her eyes bright with admiration. "Keezia's a *real* independent woman."

They resumed their shopping expedition a short time later. Phoebe had made a long prioritized list of all the items she needed to replace in the wake of the fire and was methodically working her way down it. While Lauralee seemed impressed by her organization—"Grammy Miller shops exactly the same way," she'd observed at one point—it was obvious that the teenager favored a more spontaneous approach to spending money.

"Oh, Phoebe, look!" she exclaimed as they crossed into the lingerie department of one of the mall's largest stores. "Isn't this the most gorgeous thing you've ever seen?"

"This" was an exquisite nightgown and robe set made of apricot silk. The nightgown was a floor-length sluice of fabric held up by fragile spaghetti straps. The wrap-style robe was long-sleeved and came with a matching tie belt.

"Lovely," Phoebe agreed, fingering the shimmering silk.

"It's your size, isn't it? Why don't you try it on?"

"Me?" The notion struck Phoebe as absurd. She slept in oversize cotton T-shirts. "No, I don't think—"

"It'd be *perfect* with your colorin'."

"Lauralee—"

"It's even on sale!" The girl pointed triumphantly to the price tag that dangled from the sleeve of the robe. "Look, Phoebe."

Phoebe looked. She couldn't help herself.

Hmm. Fifty percent off.

"Just try it on," Lauralee urged.

"Oh, Lauralee, it's really not me."

It really wasn't. Not at all.

Phoebe tried the apricot silk nightgown and robe on anyway.

Then she bought them.

Jackson took a sip of strong black coffee and studied the woman sitting opposite him. She was wearing a short-sleeved shirtwaist dress with a button-down collar. Her red hair was pulled back into a smooth coil at her nape. She looked cool. Calm. Very much under control.

Less than an hour ago, this same woman had been disheveled and sweaty after a long hard run. She'd come jogging up his driveway just moments after he'd pulled in. The sight of her had triggered what was becoming a very familiar stirring in the area a few inches below his belt buckle.

Well, no, that wasn't quite accurate. Something—call it anticipation, for lack of a better term—had been stirring in that general vicinity during most of his drive home from the fire station.

"So, you just made up your mind and did it, hmm, Phoebe?" he asked, setting down his coffee mug.

Phoebe patted her mouth with her napkin, then crumpled the napkin and dropped it onto the table next to her plate. "It wasn't an impulsive decision, Jackson," she said. "I thought it through."

"Oh, I'm sure you did," he returned, wondering about the faintly defensive edge he heard in her voice. "Still, to pull up stakes the way you did and move down here..."

Jackson was fishing and he knew it. For all the encounters he'd had with Phoebe since she'd taken up residence under his roof, she remained very much of an enigma to him. An extremely appealing enigma, to be sure. But an enigma nonetheless.

His red-haired, green-eyed tenant had an uncanny knack for deflecting personal inquiries. Indeed, she was so skilled at it that he hadn't even picked up on what was happening until the third time they'd had breakfast together. And once he *had* picked up on it, he hadn't been sure what to do to alter the situation.

That Phoebe's training as a psychiatrist had a lot to do with her ability to subtly distance herself seemed obvious to Jackson. At the same time, he was ready to concede that his own male ego probably made it relatively easy for her to keep the conversational focus on him. What could he say? Like a great many men, he was more than eager to accept an invitation to talk about himself. And when that invitation came from an attractive, intelligent woman...

"The job here in Atlanta was a terrific opportunity," Phoebe said. She checked her wristwatch. Jackson had the feeling that she did so not because she was worried about the time but because it offered her an excuse to evade his gaze. "Besides. There really wasn't anything to hold me in Boston."

Jackson let this last comment resonate for a few moments. He knew that Phoebe had lost both her parents. Her relationship with her father apparently had been very close. Her relationship with her mother, anything but. He also knew she'd once been engaged and that her fiancé had been killed in an accident. Exactly how the man had died and how it had affected Phoebe, Jackson couldn't say.

Yet.

"Phoebe—" he began, then stopped as he heard the squeak of a floorboard. He had no doubt what the sound signified.

If Phoebe registered the noise, she gave no sign of it. Instead, she gave him a quick smile and pushed her chair back from the table. "I have to go to work now, Jackson," she said. "Thanks for another delicious breakfast. If you'd like to run with me tomorrow morning—"

"I would," he answered quickly. Then, as she started to get to her feet, he reached across the table and caught her hand. She looked at him, eyes wide. Jackson wondered whether she'd experienced the same jolt of connection he'd felt when his fingers had closed around hers. When he resumed speaking, his voice was husky. "I'd also like to have dinner with you tomorrow night."

"Dinner?" Phoebe pronounced the word as though it were an alien concept to her. "You mean . . . here?"

"No. Out somewhere."

"Would, ah, Lauralee—?"

Jackson heard another squeak. "She has other plans."

"Well . . ." She tried to free her fingers. He didn't let go.

"I'm not going to take no for an answer, Phoebe."

Her chin notched up, just the way he'd expected it would. "Oh, really?"

"Really." Jackson waited a beat, then let his mouth relax into a smile. He released Phoebe's hand. Slowly. Very slowly. "But I will say please a bunch of times if that'll help persuade you."

He knew he'd won when he saw Phoebe bite her lower lip to prevent herself from laughing. He was taken aback by the surge of relief he felt. He'd never had to plead for female companionship. In point of fact, there'd been a few times in his life when he would have expired from exhaustion if he'd accepted everything that had been offered to him.

"Let's hear you say it, then," Phoebe challenged.

He did. Twice.

Lauralee wandered into the kitchen less than a minute after Phoebe left for the hospital. She made a great show of yawning and knuckling her eyes.

"'Morning, Lauralee," Jackson said. "Just getting up?"

The yawning stopped. So did the eye-knuckling. Several moments slipped by. Jackson watched, amused, as his daughter decided how to respond to his opening gambit. He sensed she was tempted to try to brazen things out. Ultimately, however, she opted to come clean.

"You knew I was listenin', didn't you, Daddy," she said with a sigh.

"'Fraid so, sugar. Let me give you a little hint. Squeaky floorboards and eavesdropping do not go together."

"I wasn't *eavesdroppin'*," Lauralee disputed. "At least, not on purpose." She crossed to the kitchen table and plunked herself down in the chair where Phoebe had been sitting. "I mean, I didn't know Phoebe was havin' breakfast with you. Not at first. Then when I realized, I decided it'd be rude to interrupt."

"Very considerate."

There was a pause. Then she said, "In case you're wonderin', I think it's a good idea."

"What's that?"

Lauralee's mouth curled into a satisfied—some might even say smug—little smile. "Your takin' Phoebe out to dinner tomorrow night."

"Glad to hear it, sugar." And Jackson was. Very few of the women he'd gone out with in the years since Anne's death had found favor in his daughter's eyes.

There was another pause. Lauralee's smile faded and her expression turned serious. She fidgeted for several seconds, then fixed him with a solemn, blue-eyed stare and said, "There's just one thing."

Jackson lifted a brow, speculating about exactly what that one thing might be. The look on his daughter's pretty face made him slightly uncomfortable. It was so...so...well, "adult" wasn't precisely the word he wanted, but it was definitely somewhere in the neighborhood.

He could recall a time when his little girl had gazed up at him with uncritical adoration. She'd once whispered to him that he was her special hero. And now...

"Phoebe's not like your other dates, Daddy," Lauralee declared earnestly. "She's an independent woman. And, well, um, I'm not sayin' you're a male chauvinist or anythin'—"

"Thanks for that," Jackson interpolated, stung. That his fifteen-year-old daughter felt impelled to offer him advice about his social life was one thing. That she apparently felt it necessary to tippy-toe around his masculine ego while doing so was entirely another matter.

Lauralee smiled sweetly, then went on. "The thing you have to understand, Daddy, is that independent women have special needs...."

Five

Phoebe lifted her wineglass and studied the man sitting opposite her from beneath half-lowered lashes. She'd never seen Jackson Miller in a jacket and tie before. The change of wardrobe was taking a little bit of getting used to. For reasons she couldn't explain, she found his comparatively formal attire made her even more aware of his physique than she usually was.

"So, Phoebe." Her dining companion paused to spear the last shrimp from his seafood appetizer. "Tell me about your needs."

Phoebe nearly choked on a mouthful of the excellent Chardonnay Jackson had ordered to accompany their meal.

"I—I beg your pardon?" she finally managed to get out. She swiftly assured herself that there was no way Jackson could have said what she thought she'd heard him say. No way in the world.

Her *needs?*

She must have misunderstood him. After all, the casually elegant restaurant in which they were eating was full of people. The place was quite noisy. There was the hustle of the serving staff. The clink of silverware against china. The buzz of multiple conversations. It would be very easy for her to mistake one word for another. Jackson probably had asked her to tell him about her, ah . . . her, ah . . .

Her knees.

Yes. Yes! That had to be it. Jackson had asked her to tell him about her *knees*. Why, just a few days ago, she'd mentioned to him that she'd been having a touch of trouble with her knees when she ran. And he'd been very sympathetic. He'd even offered some suggestions about what she might do to relieve the problem. It was only natural that he'd want to find out whether she'd taken his advice.

Wasn't it?

Jackson popped the shrimp between his teeth, chewed and swallowed. The left corner of his mobile mouth kicked up suddenly, bringing one of his dimples into play. A provocative gleam appeared in the depths of his compelling eyes.

Phoebe shifted involuntarily in her seat and crossed her legs. The skirt of the black silk dress she had on whispered against the nylon of her sheer panty hose. She moistened her lips with a quick dart of her tongue, trying to ignore the fluttering sensation in the pit of her stomach.

Maybe Jackson *had* said needs after all.

"Lauralee overheard part of our conversation yesterday morning," he explained smoothly. "After you left, she came into the kitchen and she and I had a father-daughter chat. Or maybe I should call it a daughter-father chat, since she did most of the talking. In any case, Lauralee wanted me to know that she thought my taking you out to dinner was a good idea. She also wanted to make sure I understood a couple of things before I did."

"Which were?"

"That you're an independent woman and that independent women have special needs." The gleam in Jackson's eyes became brighter. His voice took on a wry hint of self-deprecation. "I got the distinct impression that my daughter doesn't think I have a snowball's chance in hell of figuring out what those needs are, much less doing anything about them. That's why I decided to ask.''

Phoebe shifted her position again. The ''independent woman'' phrase was vintage Lauralee. But where had the ''needs'' part come from? While she and Jackson's daughter had had several frank discussions during the past few weeks, the issue of her needs—as an independent woman or otherwise—had not been on the agenda.

''Are you serious?''

''Do you think I'd make something like this up?''

Phoebe considered the possibility. That Jackson was having a little fun at her expense—and his own—was obvious. Even so...

''No. Not really,'' she admitted. She took a quick sip of wine. The temperature in the restaurant seemed to have gone up several degrees during the last minute or so. ''What did you say to Lauralee when she, uh—?''

''Not much. As I told you, she did most of the talking. I was too busy trying to pick my jaw up off the floor to offer any snappy repartee.'' Jackson shook his head. ''Who knows what the conversation would have turned into if the phone hadn't rung.''

''A lecture on safe sex?''

The suggestion, flippant and unthinking, just slipped out. Jackson gave Phoebe a sharp, almost shocked, look. Appalled by her lack of control—she'd been trained to use her brain before engaging her mouth, for heaven's sake!—she began to stammer an apology.

''Jackson, I—I didn't mean—''

She got no further. To her astonishment, Jackson started to chuckle. The sound was rich and robust.

''A lecture on safe sex,'' he repeated, his voice husky with humor. ''Oh, Lord. You're probably right.'' After chuckling a bit more, he grew reflective. His gaze seemed to turn inward. He gave the impression that he was envisioning how the scenario Phoebe had suggested might play out. Finally he refocused his eyes and looked across the table. There was a wry twist to his lips. ''You know, I don't think I would have handled that very well.''

The admission surprised Phoebe as much as the laughter, maybe even a little more than. One of the most striking things about Jackson Miller was his self-confidence. So many of the men she knew seemed to be consumed by insecurity. They frequently appeared to be second-guessing themselves or trying to overcompensate for some deep-seated sense of inadequacy. Jackson, on the other hand, projected an unshakable aura of assurance. Not arrogance. It was more subtle than that. He simply behaved like a man who was utterly comfortable with himself.

Whether he'd been endowed with this inner certainty at birth or acquired it through years of putting his life on the line and surviving, Phoebe didn't know. Whatever the case, it was difficult for her to imagine him being at a loss in any situation.

Of course, if that situation involved his fifteen-year-old daughter attempting to counsel him about contemporary sexual etiquette . . .

"I'm sure you would have managed just fine, Jackson," Phoebe said, meaning it.

A crooked smile. "Maybe. But I'd just as soon not have to find out."

There was a brief silence. Phoebe picked up her fork and fiddled with the mixed green salad she'd ordered as her first course. Jackson finished his seafood appetizer and drank some wine.

"Lauralee admires you a lot," he eventually observed. "It's been 'Phoebe this' and 'Phoebe that' almost from the moment she met you."

"Do you mind?"

Jackson appeared taken aback by the question. He shook his head. "Lord, no. Not at all."

"She's a wonderful girl, Jackson."

"You really think so?"

"Yes. Of course." Phoebe put down her fork. "Don't you?"

Jackson ran the tip of his index finger around the rim of his wineglass. "I'm prejudiced. I think Lauralee's perfect."

Phoebe waited for the inevitable caveat. When it didn't come, she gently prompted, "But?"

A rueful sigh, punctuated by a grimace. "But, I worry about her. I mean, sometimes it seems like just yesterday that my daughter was crawling around in diapers, drooling and trying to say da-da. And now..."

"And now she's wearing high heels and makeup and talking about independent women and their special needs."

"You've heard this lament before, I take it?"

"Variations."

"Do all fathers—?"

"A lot of them." Phoebe smiled. "Especially the good ones."

Jackson smiled back. "Thanks for that."

"You're welcome."

Their waiter materialized at that moment and inquired whether they were done with their first courses. Receiving an affirmative, he quickly cleared their plates. After promising he'd be right back with their entrées, he bustled off.

"It works both ways, you know," Phoebe commented.

"What?"

"The worrying."

Jackson went still and stiff. An odd look passed over his face. His eyes darkened to a shadowed, twilight blue. "Are you saying Lauralee's worried about me?"

Phoebe hesitated, uncertain how to interpret his response. At the same time, she didn't want to betray Lauralee's confidences. After a few seconds she said, "Lauralee's a little concerned about how you're going to react when she turns sixteen."

Jackson's expression cleared, the tension seeped out of his leanly powerful body. "Oh." His mouth curved upward, causing his dimples to indent deeply in both cheeks. "That."

"Yes. That." Phoebe wondered fleetingly what he'd thought she'd meant. "She's not sure what's going to happen when she starts dating."

"That's easy." Jackson leaned back in his seat. "Nothing."

Phoebe blinked. "What?"

"Nothing's going to happen when Lauralee starts dating. Because any boy who shows up to take her out is going to have to have a little talk with me first. I'm going to look every one of them straight in the eye and say, 'Son, I know exactly what you want because it's the same thing I wanted when I was your age. But if you'd like a chance to reach the age I am now, you won't even consider trying to get what you want from my daughter.'" Jackson paused, seeming to consider his paternal strategy. When he resumed speaking, there was a devilish glint in his eyes. "Then I'll probably crush a few beer cans with my bare hands or offer to show the kid my shotgun collection—depending on how big he is."

If it hadn't been for the glint in the eye, Phoebe might have taken him seriously. Jackson had the overprotective papa routine down pat. She experienced a passing twinge of sympathy for Lauralee's prospective suitors, then laughed. "I have a hunch that *might* be the sort of reaction your daughter's concerned about," she advised.

Jackson feigned surprise. "Too strong?"

Phoebe held up a hand, thumb and forefinger a few millimeters apart. "Just a touch."

"Hmm. How about if I forget the shotgun collection part?"

"Do you actually *have* a shotgun collection?"

"No. But I've been considering starting one ever since the day Lauralee told me my mother had taken her shopping for a bra."

Phoebe laughed again. Jackson joined in this time. Their eyes met and Phoebe felt a honeyed warmth flood through her. Their shared laughter trailed off, leaving a charged silence.

"I really don't think you have to worry about Lauralee," Phoebe said after several seconds, hoping her voice didn't sound as throaty to him as it did to her. "She's smart. She's sensible. She has a very strong sense of who she is."

"I know," Jackson responded. "All things considered, she's probably got her head screwed on a lot straighter than I did when I was in my teens." He paused, eyeing Phoebe speculatively. Eventually he asked, "How did *your* father react the first time you went out on a date?"

Phoebe's breath caught at the top of her throat. She averted her eyes. It was one thing to tell an engaging teenage girl about her ugly duckling adolescence. It was something entirely different to be forced to admit the unpleasant truth to a man she strongly suspected had been at the top of the popularity heap throughout his high school career.

"Phoebe?"

She looked back at Jackson, firmly reminding herself that what was past was past. "Actually," she said, "my father didn't find out until a couple of weeks after it happened."

Jackson's brows came together. "He didn't find out—"

At that moment, their waiter swooped in. "Here we go," he announced cheerfully, placing a pair of artfully garnished plates on the table. "That's grilled red snapper with tropical fruit salsa for you, ma'am, and spit-roasted chicken with sauce piquante for you, sir."

There was a pause. The waiter's gaze bounced from Jackson to Phoebe and back again.

"Ah, is there a problem?" he ventured tentatively.

"No, not at all," Jackson said. "Thank you very much."

"This looks wonderful," Phoebe added, picking up her fork.

The waiter flashed a relieved smile. "Enjoy."

She'd done it again, Jackson realized with a combination of admiration and exasperation as he speared one of the spicy morsels of chicken remaining on his plate. Somehow, in the wake of the interruption by their waiter, Phoebe Donovan had steered the conversation away from herself and back to him.

Not that he hadn't aided and abetted her with just about every syllable he'd uttered during the past forty-five minutes or so. One question—she'd asked him just *one* question about the psychology of firefighting!—and he'd been off and yammering like a man who'd just been released from solitary confinement.

Lord. He couldn't believe he'd actually brought up the subject of "snotty" smoke. And he hadn't just mentioned it in passing, either. Oh, no. He'd given his dinner companion a very vivid explanation of what happened to firefighters who were unfortunate enough to inhale such smoke. At least he'd had the good sense to stop himself before he'd launched into the story about the time Fridge Randall had accidentally stepped on a—

Never mind about that.

Did Phoebe know what she was doing? Jackson wondered. Was she deliberately avoiding his questions? Consciously evading his efforts to learn more about her?

Just a day ago, he would have said yes. Definitely yes. He was no longer so certain. In fact, he was beginning to think that Phoebe's emotional defenses ran so deep she didn't even realize how consistently she sidestepped personal inquiries.

Which led to one of the biggest personal inquiries of all. *What in the name of heaven did she have to be defensive about?*

Nothing. As far as he knew, absolutely nothing.

Then again, what he knew about the red-haired, green-eyed lady psychiatrist from Boston could probably be engraved on the head of a pin and still leave plenty of room for the Ten Commandments and the Declaration of Independence. No matter that she'd been living in his house for a month. Phoebe was as elusive as mercury when it came to providing anything more than basic information about herself.

Jackson grimaced. He didn't even know why his lack of knowledge bothered him so much!

All right. All right. He was physically attracted to her. Despite the fact that she was not his usual type, something about her got to him at a very primitive level. That something had grabbed him the first moment he'd laid eyes on her and it had yet to indicate that it was going to let go anytime in the immediate future. As a matter of fact, its grip seemed to be getting tighter.

A *lot* tighter, if the truth be told. He'd actually come close to embarrassing himself during a couple of their recent morning runs. Fortunately the gym shorts he wore were baggy enough to disguise the obvious.

So, he was attracted to her. Fine. Dandy. He wasn't going to deny it. But he wasn't going to do anything about it, either. At least, not anything... serious. The arguments for exercising restraint were numerous.

To begin with, Dr. Phoebe Donovan was his tenant. His closer-than-next-door neighbor.

Convenient? Undoubtedly.

Complicated? Inevitably.

To put it bluntly, he wasn't looking for long-term involvement with anyone. He'd had a wife. He'd loved her dearly. He'd lost her long before her time. It had taken him a while, but he'd finally come to terms with that.

Because of what he'd shared with Anne, he harbored a lot of warm feelings about the institution of marriage. Still, he had no desire to commit himself to it again. He made that crystal clear to the women he saw socially—*especially* to the oh-so-eligible ones who'd been pitchforked into his path by his mother during the past few years. A little no-strings fun was fine. Anything more than that...no, thank you, ma'am.

To have an affair with a woman who was paying money to occupy part of his house struck Jackson as being the antithesis of "no-strings fun."

Which brought him another crucial reason why acting on his attraction to Phoebe would be a very unwise idea. That reason was his daughter, Lauralee.

While Jackson wasn't about to pretend he'd been a monk since Anne's death, he'd been damned discreet about his social life. He didn't intend to change that. It would be a little difficult to be "discreet" with a woman who was, essentially, living under the same roof as his only child.

It was interesting, he reflected tangentially, that Lauralee had taken such an immediate and unequivocal shine to Phoebe. And there was no doubt in his mind that Phoebe genuinely liked Lauralee. In fact, he got the impression that she often preferred his daughter's company to his.

And yet ...

Jackson reached for his wineglass as his thoughts veered abruptly into dangerous territory. He raised it to his lips and took a deep drink.

Dammit! He *knew* Phoebe was as sexually aware of him as he was of her. There was no way he'd believe the electricity flowed in only one direction. He'd felt her tremble at his touch. He'd heard her breathing pattern change, seen the sudden pulsing of the vein at the base of her throat every time he got close to her. So why did she keep shutting him out? *Why?*

Maybe because she was as mixed up as he was about what was or wasn't—what should or shouldn't be—going on between them?

He certainly couldn't accuse Phoebe of leading him on. If she'd been bent on casting out lures, she would have worn her red-gold hair long and loose this evening. She also would have put on an outfit that showed off a lot more of her lithe curves and apparently flawless skin.

Of course, he had to admit that there was something intriguing about her coiffure. It gave him the feeling that if he pulled out precisely the right bobby pin, the elegantly upswept style would come tumbling down around her slender throat and shapely shoulders like flame-colored veil. At the same time, the more he considered the demure black silk dress she was wearing, the more provocative it became. Its modesty seemed increasingly like a challenge.

So...maybe she *was* leading him on? And if that was the case, could her avoidances and evasions be part of some subtle, male-female game she was playing with him?

No. He couldn't believe that of Phoebe. Nor could he accept the notion that her questions about his profession were some type of ploy. Lord, when he remembered the expression she'd worn a few minutes earlier as she'd listened to him talk about how it felt to pull up in front of a burning building and know—

"Jackson?"

The sound of his name brought Jackson out of his convoluted reverie with a start. His right hand jerked, narrowly missing his wineglass. He looked across the table at Phoebe, wondering how long he'd been trapped in the labyrinth of his thoughts.

"Is something wrong?" she asked.

"No," he replied quickly, shaking his head to underscore the point. "I was just thinking what a good listener you are."

Her eyes widened a bit. He'd been right when he'd guessed they were gold-flecked green. He would have been right if he'd guessed they held touches of brown as well.

"Thank you," she said after a moment. Her tone was guarded. So was her expression.

"I suppose you have to be, given what you do for a living."

"Well . . ."

"You don't seem very comfortable when it comes to reciprocity, though."

Phoebe frowned. "What do you mean, reciprocity?"

"Well, you encourage me to run off at the mouth about myself, but you redirect the conversation whenever I ask about you."

Although she seemed genuinely surprised, she didn't dispute his characterization of her behavior. "I . . . I didn't realize. There's not really that much for me to say about myself, Jackson. I assumed—" She paused for several seconds, then made an eloquent, openhanded gesture. "What do you want to know?"

The word "everything" trembled on the tip of Jackson's tongue. He forced himself to swallow it. Since Phoebe seemed so interested in his profession, he decided to begin by delving into hers.

"Why psychiatry?" he asked simply.

Phoebe considered the inquiry for a moment or two then answered, "I suppose it has a lot to do with following in my father's footsteps."

"He was a psychiatrist?"

"Uh-huh."

"He encouraged you to go into the field?"

"Only after I showed an interest in it. And even then, he was very candid about how tough a career it would be. He didn't try to sugarcoat anything."

"What about your mother?"

"What about her?" The question was stiff. So, very suddenly, was Phoebe's posture.

Careful, Jackson warned himself. "Did she encourage you, too?"

Phoebe glanced away. The reaction appeared to be a totally instinctive one. After a moment, she seemed to become aware of what she'd done. She looked back at him.

"My mother wasn't around," she told him. "She left when I was six."

Jackson didn't need a medical degree from Harvard to know that he'd inadvertently probed a very painful wound. "I'm sorry," he said sincerely. "I had no idea. Lauralee mentioned something about you telling her your mother died when you were eighteen—"

"She did. And my father died of a heart attack four years ago. He was playing tennis. One second he was racing for a ball and the next he was . . . he was on the ground. . . ."

A chill went up Jackson's spine. "You were there?"

"I was watching."

"Dear Lord."

"There was nothing anyone could do. The man he was playing with was a cardiac specialist. He tried CPR. But he knew there was no hope. I think I knew, too, when I saw my father fall. It was like . . . like a tree, toppling." Phoebe shook her head, her mouth curving into a bittersweet smile. "He was crazy about tennis. He said it helped him relax. Although, if you'd ever seen him on the court—"

"An all-out player, hmm?"

"I think he fantasized he was a combination of Jimmy Conners and John McEnroe. He even argued line calls."

"I know it's not much comfort, but he did die doing something he loved."

"True." She studied him for several moments. "I suppose you could say the same about your father."

It was something Jackson had thought about a great deal during the past twenty years. "No supposing," he said. "Firefighting was my daddy's life."

"Did he want you to be a firefighter, too?"

"You know, it's kind of funny. As much as the job meant to him, I'm not really sure."

It was some time before Jackson realized that Phoebe had done it to him—again.

That was when he decided that if he truly wanted to get to know his tenant, he'd better find a more effective method than asking her questions.

"Ah—Jackson?"

"Yes, ma'am?"

Phoebe glanced around, trying to orient herself. "This isn't your house we're parked in front of."

"I know" came the calm reply. "My house is about a block back. The white one with the light on in the front bedroom on the second floor."

Phoebe didn't see what this last observation had to do with anything and, after a moment or two of pondering it, she said as much.

"The front bedroom on the second floor is Lauralee's," Jackson explained succinctly. "She waited up for us."

"Oh, really?"

"She was peering out the window when I drove by the house."

Phoebe opened her mouth to make some response. Exactly what she intended to say, she could never recall. But whatever it was, it wedged in her throat when she heard the metallic click of a seat belt buckle being released. Since *her* seat belt was still very securely fastened . . .

Jackson shifted his body so he could look her squarely in the eye. Then he eased closer. Slowly. Very slowly. He reached forward.

A moment later, there was a second metallic click.

Phoebe's pulse accelerated as she felt the abrupt easing of the safety harness that ran from her shoulder to her hip and across her waist. Her breathing pattern ruffled, then turned ragged. A quicksilver combination of emotions—more intense than anticipation, less extreme than alarm—skittered through her. The air seemed to quiver, as though electrified by a lightning strike.

She said Jackson's name. Aloud. At least, she thought she did. But she wouldn't be willing to swear to it under oath.

His face was shadowed, much as it had been the first time they'd met. Now, however, her imagination was more than up to the task of supplying the details she couldn't make out.

The expression in his sky-colored eyes . . .

The set of his compelling features . . .

The very masculine curving of his sensually shaped mouth . . .

He lifted his right hand and caressed her face. The contact made her toes curl. He stroked her cheek, then let his fingertips drift downward to trace the line of her jaw. Everywhere he touched, she tingled.

"Jackson." This time she definitely did speak his name aloud. But the voice she used wasn't one she'd readily identify as her own.

"The reason I parked here instead of in front of my own house is that I've never kissed an independent woman with special needs good-night before," he told her huskily. "I'd just as soon not have an audience if I don't get it right the first time. I'm sure—" he cupped her chin and tilted it up, his callused palm firm against her skin "—you—" he leaned forward "—understand."

His breath misted across her mouth as he uttered the last word in a velvet-soft whisper. A heartbeat later, he dipped his head and claimed her lips with his own.

Phoebe made a sound—half protest, half plea—deep in her throat.

This wasn't what she . . .

There were so many reasons why they shouldn't . . .

Oh. *Oh.* Sweet heaven.

Her eyelids fluttered down. Her arms flowed up of their own volition and circled Jackson's neck.

His mouth began to move against hers. Gently at first. A teasing nuzzle here. A tender nibble there. Then with increasing urgency. The nuzzle became a languidly sensual lapping. The nibble evolved into an exquisitely calibrated love bite.

Phoebe parted her lips in response to the persuasive coaxing of Jackson's tongue. She shuddered when he accepted her yielding with a potent, pleasuring stroke. Something deep within her fisted tightly, then flowered into a fiery starburst of sensation.

The kiss grew hotter. Hungrier.

Phoebe twisted, wanting to get nearer.

That achieved, she twisted again, wanting to get nearer still.

Jackson brought his left hand up to cradle the right side of her face. She tilted her head one way as he slanted his mouth the other. Their tongues coupled and clung in a sinuous act of celebration. Their breaths merged and married.

"Phoebe...darlin'..."

"Jackson...oh, Jackson..."

Later, in the middle of a shower that was frigid enough to turn his toenails blue but incapable of cooling his blood, Jackson Stuart Miller came to the conclusion that his fifteen-year-old daughter had been absolutely right.

Phoebe Irene Donovan *wasn't* like any of the other women he'd dated.

Which was fine. Because he wasn't going to date her again.

Six

The knock on Phoebe's front door came roughly fourteen hours after the sexually charged conclusion of her date with Jackson.

"Coming," she called, setting aside the professional journal she'd been skimming. Taking off the horn-rimmed glasses she sometimes wore for reading, she got up from her rented sofa and crossed to the front door of her apartment. "Who is it?" she inquired, ninety-nine-and-nine-tenths percent certain she knew the identity of her early-afternoon visitor.

"It's me, Phoebe," a familiar soprano voice informed her.

Phoebe undid the safety chain, unlocked the dead bolt and opened the door. "Hello, Lauralee."

The teenager extended a foil-wrapped plate on upturned palms. "I've been bakin'," she announced with a guileless, orthodontically embroidered smile. "I thought you might like some peach pie."

"Why, thank you," Phoebe responded, accepting the offering. She had to give the teenager credit for the pastry ploy. And for a remarkable degree of self-restraint, too. She'd been anticipating Lauralee's arrival on her threshold for hours. Anticipating it, and bracing for the onslaught of inquiries about the previous evening that inevitably would follow. "Would you like to come in for a few minutes?"

The question precipitated an artfully done show of hesitation. There was a brief interlude of lip nibbling followed by several seconds of forehead wrinkling. The capper was a deep sigh, clearly intended to indicate how *desperately* Lauralee yearned to accept Phoebe's invitation.

"Well, I don't want to pester you or anythin'," the teenager temporized, slanting a glance up through her fair, feathery lashes.

She clearly wanted to be coaxed. Amused and uneasily aware that Lauralee wasn't the only one who felt the need to sort out exactly what had happened the night before, Phoebe obliged with a reassuring, "You wouldn't be pestering me."

Another bit of lip nibbling. Then, "You're *sure?*"

"Positive."

A beaming look of pleasure. "Okay."

They engaged in some social chitchat while Phoebe served two pieces of the flaky-crusted, fruit-crammed pie and complementary glasses of icy cold milk. After a few minutes of eating and drinking, Lauralee broached the big question.

"Did you, um, have a nice time last night?" she inquired in an offhand tone.

Phoebe nodded, taking a moment to swallow a forkful of pie. Her mind suddenly flashed back to the rigged wager about her appearance that Jackson had made with his daughter. Given the sublime quality of Lauralee's baking, she decided that his attempt at cheating had been understandable.

"Yes," she eventually replied. "Very." —

Lauralee sipped her milk. She obviously was hoping that Phoebe would expand on this response. Phoebe didn't. Her

answer to the teenager's question had been honest . . . as far
as it went. And as far as it went was as far as she intended
to go with Jackson Stuart Miller's fifteen-year-old daughter.

As for the matter of how far she intended to go with the
man himself—

Forget about it, she told herself firmly. Just forget about
it!

"That's the same thing Daddy said," Lauralee finally
commented, toying with a glistening slice of peach.

Phoebe felt her pulse accelerate. She dabbed at her lips
with a paper napkin, thankful that her hand was steady. "Is
that so?"

"Uh-huh." Lauralee stared down at her plate, prodding
the piece of fruit with the tines of her fork. "I, um, woke up
early and made breakfast for him this mornin'. You know,
before he went to work. And I, um, asked him if he'd had a
nice time last night. He said yes. Very." She raised her gaze
to meet Phoebe's. "Just like you did."

"I'm glad to hear it." Phoebe was grateful that she wasn't
given to blushing. If she had been, she would have been beet
red. "That your father had a nice time, I mean."

"A *very* nice time," Lauralee emphasized. She speared
the slice of peach she'd been fiddling with and brought it to
her lips. Just before she popped it into her mouth she asked,
"Do you think you and Daddy might go out again?"

Phoebe took a quick drink of milk. A gulp, really.

"I don't know," she said after a few moments. It was a
lie. She knew very well that she wouldn't be accepting a
second invitation from Lauralee's father. To get any more
involved with Jackson would be like, well, it would be like
playing with fire! "Our seeing each other socially might get
a little, ah, complicated."

The teenager chewed and swallowed, regarding Phoebe
with an odd expression the whole while. Then she confided, "Daddy said something like that, too."

"He did?" Phoebe recognized she should be feeling relief at this revelation. Instead, she was experiencing something disturbingly close to resentment.

Damn the man! she fumed silently. Couldn't he have realized that there were going to be complications *before* he'd kissed her half senseless?

Of course, there was always the possibility that he'd foreseen the complications and kissed her in spite of them. Or... maybe he'd kissed her *because* of them! Maybe Jackson Stuart Miller was the kind of man who relished the idea of striking sparks and stoking flames.

"Yeah, he did." Lauralee scrunched up her freckle-dusted nose and sighed. "Then he told me I should mind my own business." A second sigh. "He sounded like he really meant it, too. So I changed the subject."

There was a pause in the conversation. Phoebe used it to finish her pie and milk. Lauralee did the same.

"More?" Phoebe eventually offered, not wanting the awkward silence that had fallen to solidify into something truly uncomfortable. No matter what her feelings toward Jackson were, her affection for his daughter was sincere.

Lauralee smiled and shook her head, clearly appreciating the effort to smooth over the break. "No, thanks. I'm stuffed. 'Sides, I've got to be goin'. One of my friends is havin' a pajama party tonight."

"That sounds like fun."

"Should be. And speakin' of fun..." The teenager let the words dangle, temptingly.

Warning bells went off inside Phoebe's head. "Yes?"

"Are you doin' anythin' next Saturday?"

"'Anything' covers a lot of territory, Lauralee. Why do you ask?"

"Well, I was wonderin' if you might like to go to the Show and Muster."

"To the what?"

"The Show and Muster. The fire department holds it every year at this fairground on the outskirts of the city. It's sort of a jamboree. There are rides and games. And teams from all the stations compete for the title of Fun Firefighters of the Year. But it's not just playin' around. The Show and Muster helps raise money for a really good cause—the Burn Foundation."

Phoebe drew a shuddery breath, fighting against a sickening rush of memory. "I . . . see," she said faintly.

The *Burn* Foundation.

Burn.

Burning.

Burned.

Oh, God . . .

The commuter plane crash that had taken Alan Brinkley's life had been a fiery one. Authorities had told her that her fiancé's body had been charred beyond recognition. His identity had had to be verified by dental records. The circumstances had given her nightmares for months.

Phoebe clenched her hands, only dimly registering the dig of her nails into the flesh of her palms. She wondered fleetingly whether she'd gone as pale as she felt.

Being burned was something Jackson risked every single day he went to work, she suddenly thought. He put himself in harm's way deliberately, doing battle with an elemental force. Each time he answered an alarm he faced the possibility of—

"Phoebe?" Lauralee questioned, her tone worried. "Are you all right?"

Phoebe started. Drawing on every ounce of self-discipline she had, she reined in her runaway emotions and summoned up what she hoped was a convincingly casual expression. "Oh, yes," she said. "Just fine."

"But you look kind of—"

"I'm *fine*, Lauralee. Really."

There was another pause. Then, "So, what do you think about the Show and Muster?" The teenager plainly was prepared to wheedle. "I truly hope you'll come, Phoebe. I mean, I'm goin' to Baltimore to visit my mama's family the very next week and I won't be back till around Labor Day. Then I'll be startin' school again. The Show and Muster's practically the last time I'll get a chance to spend any time with you!"

Phoebe shifted in her seat. "What does your father have to say about this?"

"Oh—" an airy gesture of dismissal "—he won't mind."

"Lauralee—"

"He won't," Jackson's daughter insisted, her pixieish features taking on a pugnacious cast. "You can even ask him."

Phoebe did precisely that, the very next morning.

She'd just finished her daily run.

He'd just arrived home at the end of another around-the-clock shift.

"Good morning...Jackson..." Phoebe huffed. She was uncomfortably conscious that the breathlessness of her greeting had as much to do with anxiety as with aerobic exertion.

"Oh, hi" came the laconic response. It was punctuated by a smile. A *brief* smile. One that offered no more than a nanosecond's worth of dimple.

Oh, hi? she repeated silently, her anxiety acquiring a bit of an edge. She plucked at the loose-fitting cotton top she was wearing. *That's it?*

"How was work?" she asked after a moment or two.

A smooth shrug. "Not bad. A couple of garbage fires. One false alarm. Two 911s. The first was a middle-aged accountant who thought he was having a heart attack. It was indigestion. The second was a pregnant woman whose husband thought he had plenty of time to get her to the hospital. She delivered twins on the Fourteenth Street exit of I-85." Jackson massaged the back of his neck, his manner oddly distracted. "How was your run?"

"Nowhere near as exciting as your shift."

Another smile. The dimple-display duration for this one was maybe a nanosecond and a half.

Something wasn't right, Phoebe decided.

This was the first time she and Jackson had encountered each other since the embrace they'd shared. Frankly she'd expected...well, she didn't know *what* she'd expected, exactly. But she was sure it hadn't been that Jackson would treat her as though absolutely nothing out of the ordinary had happened between them.

Not that what had occurred in the front seat of his car had been so significant, of course. She wasn't going to exaggerate the importance of the interlude. She understood the episode for what it was. And wasn't.

One kiss between two consenting adults.

Okay. No big deal.

No. Big. Deal.

But not *no* deal at all!

Still, if that's how Lieutenant Jackson Stuart Miller wanted to play it . . . fine. Just fine and dandy.

Squaring her shoulders, Phoebe proceeded to offer her landlord a carefully calibrated smile. Then she engaged him in a bit more conversation. Casual, commonplace conversation. The kind of conversation they'd been exchanging for weeks. Eventually—once she'd satisfied herself she'd amply demonstrated that the end-of-date embrace they'd shared had meant even less to her than it evidently had to him—she segued into the subject of Lauralee's invitation.

"The Show and Muster?" Jackson repeated, an emotion Phoebe couldn't decipher flashing through his sky-colored eyes. "Oh, sure. You'd be more than welcome to come."

His tone was cordial enough. Yet Phoebe didn't find it very persuasive. Jackson might *say* she'd be "welcome" at the Show and Muster, but she was willing to lay odds he didn't really want her to go.

For reasons she couldn't explain, her memory chose that moment to spit out a name she'd heard only once and hadn't wondered about more than three—or was it four? or maybe five?—times during the past few weeks.

Keezia Carew.

The "exotic" female whose independence Lauralee admired so much. The woman who shared Jackson's profession.

"But?" Phoebe prompted after a fractional pause.

Jackson's forehead furrowed. "But what?"

"I heard a 'but' in your voice, Jackson. About the idea of my going to the Show and Muster."

Once again, Jackson's vivid eyes glinted with an emotion Phoebe didn't know how to interpret. He rocked back on the heels of his well-polished shoes and thrust his hands into the pockets of the ink-blue trousers of his uniform. The gold-toned nameplate he wore pinned on the left side of his short-sleeved shirt caught a ray of morning sunshine.

"I'm not sure it's your sort of thing," he told her after a second or two.

Suddenly Phoebe was transported back to her awkward adolescence. To the years when everybody had been "in" and she'd been so far "out" she hadn't even been worth mocking. "You mean, I wouldn't fit in," she translated tightly.

"I didn't say that, Phoebe," Jackson countered. It was the first time during this conversation that he'd used her name. "I'm just not sure you'd enjoy it."

Phoebe made up her mind right then and there that she was going to attend the Show and Muster. "Oh, really?" she challenged, lifting her chin. "Well, Lieutenant Miller, I just might surprise you."

Actually she wound up surprising herself.

Phoebe had never been one for outdoor mob scenes. Yet she found the fairground hurly-burly of the Show and Muster both entertaining and invigorating.

She'd never been very keen on cheering from the sidelines, either. Yet she just about hollered herself hoarse as Jackson and his station colleagues proved themselves to be the best at everything from bucket brigading to hose laying and were duly designated Fun Firefighters of the Year.

"You were great, Daddy!" Lauralee enthused after the award presentation ceremony. She gave her father a big hug, then turned to Phoebe and asked, "Wasn't he great?"

"Very impressive," Phoebe responded. It had given her an odd feeling to watch Jackson demonstrating the skills of his profession. Even to her untrained eye, his proficiency had been obvious. He'd moved like a superbly trained athlete and commanded the field like a born leader. Still, all the while she'd observed and applauded, she'd been thinking about the dangers inherent in what he did.

"Thanks," Jackson said, removing his helmet and raking the fingers of one hand back through his sweat-dampened hair. Like his fellow firefighters, he was wearing his turnout gear—a dark, knee-length coat with reflective yellow stripes; heavy trousers with reinforced knees; bulky boots. Phoebe couldn't help recalling the first time she'd seen him in such cumbersome garments. His gaze met hers for a moment and she had the distinct impression that he was recalling it, too.

"Did you hear me and Phoebe cheerin' for you?" Lauralee inquired.

Jackson's eyes held Phoebe's for a split second more. Then he transferred his attention to his daughter. "I think folks in Biloxi, Mississippi, probably heard you, sugar."

"Oh, Daddy."

"It's a good thing your grandmama's not here," Jackson teased. He undid the front of his jacket. It swung open to reveal a sweat-blotched T-shirt. "If she'd heard you raising your voice like that, she'd've fainted away with mortification."

Lauralee giggled. "But first she would've given me another lecture on behavin' like a lady."

Having met Lauralee's Grammy Miller several days earlier, Phoebe found the fainting scenario farfetched. The lecturing on propriety prediction, however, sounded entirely plausible. Perfectly groomed and impeccably mannered, Louisa Miller had proven to be every bit as formidable in the flesh as she was in her photograph. Sort of a Dixie version of a middle-aged Queen Victoria. Indeed, Phoebe had had to restrain an impulse to drop a curtsy when she'd been presented to her.

Phoebe had been interested in becoming acquainted with the older woman for a number of reasons. The picture Jackson had shown her the first morning they'd had breakfast together had intrigued her, of course. And so had the biography Lauralee had sketched out several days later.

Louisa Miller, it seemed, was the daughter of wealthy, socially prominent parents. At age twenty, after having rejected proposals from several extremely eligible suitors,

she'd stunned her family and friends by falling in love with
a firefighter who'd been summoned to her college sorority
house to rescue a prize-winning Persian cat. There'd been a
battle of wills, but Louisa Lee Chastain had eventually become Mrs. Nathan Miller.

Phoebe's encounter with Lauralee's grandmother had
been an odd one. She'd been conscious of being judged. Yet
the older woman's graciousness had been such that she'd
been unable to determine whether she'd been deemed ac-
ceptable or not. Even in retrospect...

"My granddaughter tells me you're a psychiatrist at one
of our fine city hospitals, Dr. Donovan," Louisa Miller had
observed after Lauralee had performed the necessary intro-
ductions. Her voice had held an equal mix of sugar and
shrewdness.

"Yes, ma'am," Phoebe had confirmed.

"Grammy Miller thinks people who go to psychiatrists
should have their heads examined," Lauralee had interpolated with a mischievous giggle.

"Lauralee," her grandmother had reproved, her expression stern. After a moment, she'd shifted her gaze to
Phoebe. Her eyes, Phoebe had noted, were as intensely blue
as her son's. But where his had a bold, open sky quality, hers
seemed shuttered, even steely. "I apologize for my granddaughter."

"No problem," Phoebe had replied, acutely conscious
that Louisa Miller's apology had not included a repudia-
tion of the sentiments ascribed to her. She hadn't thought
the omission was accidental. "A lot of people have, ah—"
she'd paused, searching for a neutral word "—*reservations*
about psychiatry."

The older woman had frowned, ever so slightly. Phoebe
had gotten the impression that she didn't like being lumped
in with "a lot of people."

"I'm well aware that your profession can be extremely
useful in certain cases, of course," Louisa Miller had declared after a tiny pause. Her tone had suggested that she
couldn't envision herself having anything to do with one of
these cases. "It's just that, well, perhaps it's the way I was

brought up, Dr. Donovan, but I can't help thinking that people would be better off discussing their problems with their families or friends rather than going to some *stranger*."

Phoebe had conceded the point, then added, "Unfortunately the problems most people want to discuss when they seek psychiatric help center on their families or friends or a combination of both. Sometimes going to a stranger is the only—"

A bass voice jolted Phoebe out of her ruminations about Jackson's mother.

"Hey, man! Are we the best, or are we the *best?*"

The ebullient inquiry came from a massively built, magnificently mustachioed black man who'd materialized beside Jackson sometime in the last few seconds. He was dressed in jeans and an orange T-shirt emblazoned with the words Hot Stuff.

Phoebe caught her breath. She'd noticed this particular man during the Fun Firefighter competition. It would have been impossible not to, given his size. But what had riveted her attention had been his interaction with Jackson. She'd known, instantly, that she'd seen him before.

It had taken her a moment to realize when . . . and where. An image she'd done her best to obliterate had suddenly crystallized in her mind's eye.

There were two helmeted and heavily garbed firefighters standing together just up ahead of her. One was white. He was tall and broad-shouldered. The other was black. He was just plain huge. Something about the two men communicated the message that they were bonded by friendship as well as a common profession.

"We are *definitely* the best," Jackson said. There was an enthusiastic exchange of high-five hand slaps.

"You were both terrific," Lauralee chimed in.

The man gave her a wink. "I did my best to make your daddy look good." He inclined his head toward Phoebe. "I didn't want him to embarrass himself in front of Dr. Donovan, here."

That the firefighter knew who she was was a surprise. Phoebe slanted a quick glance at Jackson. While the expression on his face was impossible to read, it seemed to her the color in his cheeks was higher than it had been a few seconds earlier.

He'd been talking about her, Phoebe thought. Jackson had been talking about her to his friend. But *why?* And what had he said?

Had Jackson told him about the kiss? she wondered. He'd never spoken about it to her. And he certainly hadn't tried for a second. Indeed, in the wake of their off-kilter encounter in his driveway the morning after Lauralee had invited her to the Show and Muster, their relationship had reverted to the same pleasant—and emphatically platonic—pattern to which it had conformed before they'd had their first date.

Well, no. Perhaps not precisely the same. She was willing to admit that she'd experienced a certain degree of, ah, *edginess* in Jackson's presence since their dinner date. And there'd been times when she'd sensed he felt a similar kind of tension, too. But beyond that...

"Phoebe, meet Ralph Randall," Jackson said, gesturing. "Fridge, meet Dr. Phoebe Donovan."

"Fridge?" Phoebe repeated, looking up at the man. He was well over six feet tall and had a shoulder span a pro football player would covet. "You're...Fridge?"

She'd heard the name at least a dozen times since she'd moved into the Miller house. Based on what had been said in connection with the name, she'd swiftly come to the conclusion that her initial speculation—that Fridge might be a source of friction between Jackson and Lauralee—had been totally wrong.

"That's right," Fridge affirmed. He put out his right hand. Phoebe didn't so much accept it as extend her own hand and allow it to be engulfed and shaken. "My friends call me Fridge because I'm so cool."

"His friends call him Fridge because a couple of years ago we had a bunch of kindergartners come to the station house on a field trip and this one little kid took a good long gander at him and squeaked out, 'Gee, Mr. Fireman, you're even bigger than my mama's 'fridg-idator,'" Jackson corrected.

Fridge waited a beat then blandly inquired, "Did this peewee white boy ever tell you about the time he saved the life of his shift captain, Dr. Donovan?"

There was an anticipatory giggle from Lauralee.

"Make it Phoebe, Fridge, please," Phoebe requested. "And no, Jackson hasn't gotten around to telling me that particular story."

"I didn't think so," Fridge replied with a sorrowful shake of his head. "What with him bein' so modest and all."

Phoebe suppressed a smile. "I don't suppose you'd consider—?"

Fridge maintained his pseudo-solemn demeanor. "Well, Phoebe," he began with the intonation of an accomplished raconteur, "it happened about fourteen years ago. Just a couple of weeks after Jackson graduated the fire academy and was assigned to his first station house. Now I wasn't real well acquainted with him at the time, you understand. But I'd picked up on his reputation. I mean, everybody knew he was the most gung-ho probationary firefighter in the history of the department. Used to sleep in his turnout gear so he'd be the first one ready when an alarm went off. Practiced holdin' his breath till his face turned purple and his eyes bulged out, just in case he ever got caught short of air. That sort of thing."

Phoebe glanced at Jackson. The expression on his tanned, lean-featured face hinted that Fridge's description wasn't too far off the mark. It also suggested he found the evocation of his younger, gung-ho self a bit embarrassing. After a moment, she returned her attention to Fridge. "I think I get the idea," she said, smiling encouragingly. "What happened?"

He smiled back at her, his even white teeth gleaming beneath his thick mustache. "Well, Jackson's station caught the alarm on an apartment fire. The word at the scene was, there might be somebody stuck inside. So, naturally, Probie Miller went chargin' right in, humpin' hose and searchin' for the unfortunate occupant. Problem was, he couldn't see anythin'. I mean, the place was full of smoke. Real thick, snot—ah, I mean—''

''Phoebe knows all about snotty smoke, Fridge,'' Jackson interpolated wryly.

The big firefighter lifted his brows, apparently surprised by this bit of information. Phoebe saw a look she couldn't interpret pass between him and Jackson. After a second, Fridge cleared his throat and went on with his story.

''So, okay,'' he said. ''There was smoke everyplace. And in the middle of it there was Probie Miller, feelin' his way around. Feelin'...feelin'...'' Fridge gestured expressively with his ham-size hands. ''Then *wham!* He smacked into what he decided had to be the resident and he nabbed him in a bear hug. But this guy tried to fight him off. Probie Miller figured he must be terrified, you know? Or maybe deranged from somethin' in the smoke. So he got an extra-good grip on the guy and started draggin' him out. Only it was a real battle. Which got young Jackson Miller just a little ticked off. I mean, if you're puttin' it on the line to rescue a guy, you're entitled to some cooperation, right?''

''Oh, absolutely,'' Phoebe concurred. She heard Lauralee giggle again. It was obvious the teenager had heard this tale many times before.

Fridge grinned broadly. ''Well, to make a long story short, Probie Miller managed to haul this highly uncooperative individual to safety. By the time he did, he was hoppin' mad. I mean, it was hot enough to fry spit and he was sweatin' like a hog. He had all kinds of disgustin' stuff oozin' out of his nose. His eyeballs probably felt like they were sittin' in sandpaper-lined sockets, too. So, he ripped off his B.A.—that's breathin' apparatus—and got set to let this guy have it. But just as he opened his mouth, he realized that his supposed apartment occupant was wearin' turnout gear. Then the guy whirled around and he saw that his supposed apartment occupant was his very own shift captain from his very own station. He also saw that this shift captain was a mite, ah, incensed. So Probie Miller stood there, his jaw flappin' in the breeze, figurin' his career with the department was toast, you know? Finally the captain reared back and roared—'' He paused dramatically, then grinned at Jackson, ceding the punchline to him.

"'If you ever save my life like that again, boy,'" Jackson quoted sardonically. "'I'll kill you.'"

"And Daddy never did," Lauralee declared triumphantly.

"Not while he was a probie, anyway," Fridge added, and gave his buddy a clap on the back that Phoebe suspected would have sent a lot of men collapsing to their knees.

Once Jackson shed and properly stowed his turnout gear, he suggested they all take a stroll around the fairground and get something to eat. About ten minutes into their ambling tour of the various Show and Muster games and displays, Lauralee spotted several of her friends from school. After receiving permission from her father, she scampered off to join them.

Phoebe, Jackson and Fridge ended up lunching at a tree-shaded picnic table. It seemed to Phoebe that the two men insisted on purchasing at least one of every type of food available from the fairground's numerous concession stands before they finally sat down. She contented herself with a mustard-slathered hot dog, a scoop of coleslaw and a large cup of icy lemonade.

She had plenty of time in which to savor her selections. Engaging in what obviously was a long-standing tradition of "I can top that," her two dining companions took turns regaling her with stories about firefighting. Their tales were very funny. Even the ones centering on moments of mortal danger were spun out in lighthearted fashion. Injuries were portrayed as inconveniences or opportunities to collect a paycheck for doing nothing. Fear was admitted to, but always in a tone that seemed to mock the emotion.

"Stop," Phoebe finally had to plead. Jackson, who was sitting next to her, had just finished recounting a hilarious anecdote about a 911 emergency rescue call that had involved an interstate collision between a tanker full of chocolate syrup and a truck carrying several dozen crates loaded with goose down. The nonstop laughter he'd provoked with his wonderfully timed delivery had left her gasping for air. She could feel tears of merriment streaming down her cheeks. "Please . . . stop."

"Oh, man, Jackson," Fridge chortled from the other side of the table. He took a swig from the condensation-fogged can of cola he was holding. "Do you remember how Chuckie Fremont wound up all over the local news that night?"

Jackson handed Phoebe a paper napkin so she could wipe her eyes. Their fingers brushed briefly as she took it, undercutting all the progress she'd made toward recovering her breath. Something deep inside her contracted. She dipped her head, not daring to speak.

"Yeah, and he made the front page of the *Atlanta Constitution*, too," Jackson said. His tone was deeper than it had been a moment before. The blue of his eyes was darker. "It looked like he'd been tarred and—"

"Let me guess," a sassy female voice interrupted. "You two fun firefighters are torturing this poor woman with the story of charging Chuckie Fremont and the chocolate syrup."

The source of this interpolation was one of the most striking women Phoebe had ever seen. She was about five foot six and appeared to be in her mid-twenties. The lushness of her lips, the texture of her dark, close-cropped hair and the burnished mocha of her skin suggested a predominantly African heritage. But there were other ethnic strains as well. Her nose was imperiously narrow, her cheekbones elegantly angular. Her eyes—which flashed like golden topazes—tilted slightly upward at the outer corners.

She was wearing a sleeveless, tightly belted yellow jumpsuit that showed off a sleekly muscular physique. Hoops of hammered metal dangled from her earlobes. She looked like something out of *Vogue*. Phoebe—who was wearing sneakers, shorts and a plain pullover top—felt downright dowdy.

"Sister Carew," Fridge said, his rumbling voice rich with affection. He got to his feet.

"Hey, Keezia." Jackson stood up, too.

Keezia Carew? Phoebe thought, stunned. *This* was Keezia Carew?

"I thought you were still in Memphis with your mama," Fridge commented.

"I drove back overnight."

"She's feelin' better, then?"

"Enough to start nagging me about when I'm going to come to my senses and settle down with you," Keezia answered flippantly. A toss of her head set her earrings swinging. After a brief pause, she shifted her attention to Phoebe and said, "Dr. Phoebe Donovan, am I right?"

Phoebe gaped. First Fridge Randall had figured out her identity. Now this extraordinary woman was addressing her by name. What in heaven's name was going on? Had Jackson turned her into the hot topic at the local fire station?

"Yes," she affirmed after a moment. She took a deep breath, drawing on her stores of professional poise. "And you're obviously Keezia Carew, the firefighter."

Keezia seemed genuinely startled. A bit suspicious, even. Her topaz gaze bounced from Phoebe to her two colleagues. "Has somebody been talking behind my back?" she demanded.

"Not me," Fridge denied, shaking his head.

"Me, either," Jackson said. He looked at Phoebe. "How the heck did you—?"

"Lauralee," Phoebe informed him, then turned back toward the woman firefighter. For reasons she couldn't begin to articulate, she felt a sudden affinity with Keezia. Although she'd always been slow to make female friends, something told this circumstance was about to change.

"Jackson's daughter, Lauralee, mentioned your name to me," she explained. "She's a big admirer of yours, Ms. Carew. She thinks you're a very independent woman."

There was a peculiar silence. Eventually, Phoebe heard Fridge mutter what sounded a lot like an affirmation of Lauralee's assessment of Keezia's character. His tone suggested he would have preferred being able to take issue with it.

Keezia gave a throaty laugh. "Well, I guess that's one way to describe me," she acknowledged. She eyed Phoebe with disconcerting directness for several moments, then cocked her head and drawled, "But you know something? I'm willing to bet *you're* pretty independent, too."

Seven

Phoebe wanted him.

Jackson could see it in the gold-sparked heat of her emerald eyes and the passion-fueled rosiness of her delicate skin.

He could feel it in the tantalizing shift of her slender hips and the inviting press of her taut-tipped breasts.

"Jackson," she pleaded huskily. The feathery brush of her fingertips against his naked skin was seductive beyond words. "Please...Jackson..."

He groaned on a shudder of response. His heart was hammering, his breathing pattern breaking apart. The degree of his eagerness was adolescent. The depth of his hunger, utterly adult.

He'd waited so long for her. Evading the attraction that had existed since the first instant he'd laid eyes on her. Denying the desire that had grown more and more potent with the passage of time. Perhaps he'd been a fool to resist, but steering clear had seemed the right thing to do.

And now...

He buried his face in the silken tumble of her flame-colored hair for a moment, then nuzzled his lips against the perspiration-sheened curve of her brow. He charted her face with kisses, finally moving to claim her lips. She yielded to him with a shallow, rapturous sigh. Her arms circled his neck. He felt the clutch of her fingers in the hair on the back of his head.

Yes, he thought, caressing her from shoulder to waist, from waist to thigh. *Oh, yes.*

"Phoebe," he whispered hoarsely. "Phoebe...darlin'..."

The waiting was over. The time was ripe. And heaven knew, his need for her was no less than hers for—

And then he heard it.

Alarm.

Fire.

Jackson came awake with a jolt, adrenaline flooding his veins. For an instant, he was totally disoriented. His body was sending one message, his brain another. Then, abruptly, everything snapped into focus. Fourteen years of experience and a bred-in-the-bone sense of duty overrode the effects of the most intensely erotic dream he'd ever known.

Alarm!

Fire!

Jackson was off the narrow bunk where he'd been dreaming in a heartbeat. He scrambled into his gear, his movements swift and sure, donning protective boots and pants in a matter of seconds. Then he headed for his assigned position on the station's ladder truck, pulling on his heavy turnout coat as he went.

In the usual scheme of things, Fridge would have been striding right next to him, ready to climb up behind the tiller wheel on the rear of the truck. But Fridge was out sick, felled by a particularly virulent form of the flu that had been circulating through the department during the past week and a half. Jackson had called to check on his condition around lunchtime. Keezia Carew, who was assigned to the C-shift at the station, had answered the phone. According to her, Fridge had declared that he was going to need to recover a bit before he felt sufficiently well to die.

"Let's move it!" somebody yelled.

Jackson pulled the door on the right side of the ladder truck closed and buckled his seat belt. He checked his wristwatch. Seven minutes past four. His shift had already gone out on five calls. The last one had come in around midnight and had involved a torched automobile.

This alarm was for a fire at a wooden frame, multiple-family dwelling in one of Atlanta's more modest neighborhoods. Jackson was familiar with the area and vaguely recalled responding to a 911 call at the address during the previous Christmas holidays. He knew it was a quick trip to the place as the crow flew, a much longer one when made via narrow residential streets.

The station's engine, which carried the hoses and a tank containing several hundred gallons of water, reached the location first. That was the norm. The plugman was beginning to hook up a line to a hydrant when the truck Jackson was riding on rolled in.

"No way is this a single alarm," the driver to Jackson's left said, braking the vehicle and killing its wailing siren.

Jackson cast a practiced eye over the four-story structure. While there weren't many flames visible, the place was venting an ominous amount of smoke.

"Yeah," he agreed grimly and swung out of the cab.

He had a bad feeling about this call. A very bad feeling.

The feeling got worse when a woman—one of the several dozen civilians stumbling around the scene—started screaming.

"They left a baby!" was her anguished cry. "They left a baby inside!"

Jackson had heard many variations on these shrill words during his fourteen years on the job. Their kick-in-the-gut impact hadn't lessened over time.

They—whomever the hell "they" were—had *left* a helpless human being inside a burning building. They'd left him or her like a pair of worn-out shoes or a forgotten piece of luggage.

He shouldered his way to the screaming woman and managed to get her calmed down enough so he could extract the information he needed. Then he headed toward the structure at a quick jog. By that time, several windows had shattered outward, spewing sharp-edged shards of glass over the ground. Suddenly the incendiary enemy that had to be battled was very evident. Tongue-shaped flames licked against the star-spattered sky.

Jackson had memorized the facts. He knew that most of Georgia's fire-related fatalities occurred between eleven at night and six in the morning, when people were sleeping. He knew that nine out of ten of the victims were dead from smoke or toxic gases before the fire department was even called.

But there was always a chance...

Jackson got into what supposedly was the baby's room by squeezing through a window. Smoke enveloped him immediately. He dropped down low to the floor, sticking close to the wall and disciplining himself to breathe as normally as he could while wearing a mask. He couldn't see a thing.

He began to crawl around the room in a clockwise pattern. Keeping his left hand on the wall to maintain some sense of orientation, he stretched out his right hand and felt around.

Nothing.

He inched forward and felt again.

For one heart-stopping moment, he thought he'd found the child he was so desperately seeking. His gloved fingers closed around what seemed to be a soft little limb—

"*Mama,*" the doll he'd just grasped wailed. "*Mama.*"

Cursing, Jackson cast the toy aside and crawled on. A moment or two later, he bumped into the corner of a piece of furniture. It felt like a table. He ran his hand along the floor beneath, hoping against hope.

Nothing.

He crawled onward, conscious that the room was getting hotter. He glanced up for an instant and caught a glimpse of a reddish-gold glow.

The fire was in the ceiling. The possibility of a collapse— or, God help him, of a flashover—was very, very real.

He kept going. Head down. Hands patting the carpeted floor. Inch by inch by inch . . .

Jackson collided with another piece of furniture. It took him a moment to identify it as a crib. Praying, he hauled himself to his feet and leaned over the crib's protective railing. The bend-and-reach movement was ingrained in his muscle memory. He'd repeated it countless times when his daughter had been an infant.

Be alive, he pleaded silently. Please. Be alive.

And then . . . contact.

Jackson knew. The instant he scooped up the small, blanket-swathed body and cradled it protectively against his chest, he *knew* . . . with soul-chilling certainty.

But he didn't know everything. "Everything" had to wait until after he'd gotten outside. Until after he'd spent ten fruitless minutes performing CPR. Until after one of the emergency medical technicians had told him to stop because there was nothing he—or anybody else—could do.

The dead child Jackson had carried from the burning apartment building turned out to be a towheaded toddler who was less than two years old. Her name, according to the hysterical young woman who suddenly materialized out of the night and snatched her lifeless little body from his arms, was Anne.

Anne . . . with an *e*.

Jackson wanted her.

Phoebe could see it in the blaze of his brilliant blue eyes and the flush of sexual excitement that rode high on his sharply hewn cheekbones.

She could feel it in the ardent movements of his powerfully muscled body and in the rigid evidence of his masculine arousal.

"Phoebe," he murmured, his voice like velvet. A puff of warm breath fanned her skin. His work-hardened palms cupped the sensitive undercurves of her bared breasts. He finessed the peaking tips with the pads of his thumbs, triggering a starburst of pleasure deep within her. "Phoebe, darlin' . . ."

Emboldened as she had never been in her life, she matched his tactile provocation with her own. She explored him with avid fingers, experiencing a sense of possessiveness she would have sworn was totally alien to her nature.

Their mouths met and mated in a long, languid kiss. Tongues twined, slick and sinuous.

"Jackson," she moaned, arching against him. The tawny hair that swirled across his broad chest teased her nipples. She brought her hands up in a gliding caress and locked them around his neck. "Oh, Jackson . . . yes . . ."

She'd fought against this. Truly, she had. She'd armed herself with a veritable arsenal of shouldn'ts, wouldn'ts and couldn'ts. But the time for struggling was gone. The barriers were down. She could no longer hide from herself or from the yearning hunger that every instinct she had told her this man was destined to—

B-b-rring.

What?

B-b-rring!

A telephone.

A . . . telephone?

Phoebe surfaced from her pool of slumber-induced sensuality with shocking abruptness. Her pulse was pounding, her mind was in a whirl. For an unsettling moment, she was uncertain whether she was genuinely awake or simply dreaming she was.

B-b-rring!

The shrill summons argued persuasively for the former.

Phoebe rolled over. She reached clumsily for the cordless telephone sitting on the small table next to her bed. Her hand was shaking. She was acutely conscious that there was a throbbing ache between her thighs.

She . . . and Jackson Stuart Miller. Together. Making love.

It was only a dream! she told herself fiercely.

True. But as a psychiatrist, she recognized that dreams were often a manifestation of deep-seated—

"Hello?" she croaked into the mouthpiece of the phone. This was not the time to start analyzing the workings of her subconscious!

No answer.

"Hello?" she repeated, levering herself into a sitting position and sweeping a tangled skein of hair out of her face. She caught a glimpse of the clock that sat on her bedside table. Its digital readout declared the time to be 9:02 a.m. Normally she would have been up two hours ago. However, she'd had an emergency call involving one of her patients late the previous evening. She hadn't gotten to sleep until shortly before dawn. And once she had gotten to sleep...

"Phoebe?" The voice on the other end of the line was gruff. It sounded distorted, as though the speaker was trying to disguise it.

Phoebe stiffened. She'd been the target of crank phone-calls more than once in her medical career. "Who is this, please?" she asked sharply.

There was a raspy inhalation. "It's Fridge Randall."

"Fridge?" Fear touched her with a clammy hand. Although she'd gotten to know Jackson's good friend and fellow firefighter fairly well during the two weeks since the Show and Muster, their acquaintanceship didn't extend to chummy telephone chats. She could think of only one reason why he'd be calling her at two minutes past nine on a Sunday morning. "You sound awful!"

"Got some kind of—" a pause for a phlegmy cough "—flu bug."

Phoebe relaxed slightly. "Oh. I'm sorry to hear that. There's a virus going around the hospital, too."

"Yeah, well, it could be worse." Another cough. "Look, Phoebe. Why I'm callin'. Does Jackson happen to be there?"

A wave of heat washed over Phoebe. Her breath wedged in her throat. Finally she managed to inquire, "You mean...here? With me?"

"Yeah."

She swallowed convulsively and moistened her suddenly dry lips with a quick lick of her tongue. "No." She shook her head. "Jackson isn't here. Why would you—?"

Fridge didn't allow her to complete her question, nor did he answer it. "Do you know whether he's gotten home from work yet?"

The intensity of this inquiry sliced through Phoebe's embarrassment. "No, I don't," she said. She felt one of the spaghetti-thin straps of her nightgown—the apricot silk nightgown she'd purchased while shopping with Lauralee—slide halfway down her upper arm. Tugging it back into place, she asked, "Is something wrong, Fridge?"

"I'm—" again, a congested-sounding cough "—not sure. The station caught an alarm on an apartment fire early this morning. There was a casualty. A little girl. Jackson found her and brought her out. There wasn't a mark on her, from what I hear. But she was stone-cold gone. Smoke inhalation, probably. That's what kills most folks in a fire, not the flames."

"Oh, dear God," Phoebe whispered, horrified.

"Keezia got called to fill in at the station today," Fridge continued. "Seems about half the department's out sick. Anyway, she phoned me with the story. Said Jackson looked pretty shaken when she saw him at the shift change. The captain on duty mentioned somethin' about havin' him talk with one of the department counselors. Jackson told him no way and drove off. I thought maybe he'd stop by my place but, well . . ."

Phoebe kicked aside the bed linen and got up as Fridge's illness-roughened voice trailed off into an uneasy silence. A dozen different alarms—some personal, some professional—were jangling inside her brain. "Have you tried to reach him?" she asked, padding across the bedroom, the portable phone pressed to her right ear.

"I've been callin' his number every fifteen minutes or so since seven-thirty. All I get is an answerin' machine tellin' me to leave a message." A sneeze exploded through the line, followed by a long, snuffling inhalation. "Man, I hate those things!"

"What about his mother?" Phoebe was heading for the living room. She knew she could see the Miller driveway from one of its windows. It was entirely possible Jackson was home but not picking up his phone. "Have you contacted her?"

No reply.

"Fridge?"

"I don't believe Jackson would go to his mama with somethin' like this, Phoebe," Fridge finally replied.

The response was as cryptic as it was quiet, yet Phoebe found herself shying from the idea of asking him to elaborate on it.

I don't believe Jackson would go to his mama with somethin' like this, Phoebe.

And yet Fridge clearly believed that Jackson might bring the burden of "something like this" to *her*.

Why? Phoebe wondered. Was it because she was a psychiatrist? Or was it because—

Stop it! she told herself, chopping off what she knew was a very dangerous line of inquiry. Just stop it.

Fridge's reasons for believing what he believed weren't important. At least, not right now. The fact was, Jackson *hadn't* come to her. He hadn't sought her out for counsel or comfort or anything else. And why should he? During the past two weeks their relationship, such as it was, had settled into a pleasantly platonic friendship. Nothing more. Nothing less. If Fridge chose to read something into this friendship that didn't exist—

Stop it!

Phoebe twitched aside the curtains on the main livingroom window and peered out. Anxiety-edged disappointment caused her to tighten her grip on the telephone. "Fridge?" she asked after a moment, letting the draperies drop back into place.

"Still—" cough, sniffle, cough "—here."

"I don't see Jackson's truck. He always parks it in the driveway when he comes home from the station."

"Oh, man."

"Fridge, you don't think—" She stopped, not wanting to voice her fears. Jackson Stuart Miller was one of the strongest, most centered human beings she'd ever met. But as a psychiatrist she was well aware that even the strongest person could be made utterly weak, even the most centered individual knocked totally off balance.

"I don't know what to think. Maybe... maybe Jackson's out drivin' around, tryin' to clear his head. Maybe he stopped someplace to get some breakfast. Or maybe he went to church. That's what I'd do." Fridge gave a wheezy sigh. "He's bound to come home sooner or later. And when he does, will you give me a call? My number is—"

"Hold on," Phoebe requested, scrambling for a scrap of paper and a pencil. "Okay, go ahead."

Fridge recited seven digits, then sneezed violently several times.

Phoebe frowned, genuinely concerned by the way he sounded. "Have you been to a doctor?"

"Yeah." A pause for several seconds of nose blowing. "The man's got me poppin' antibiotics. And Keezia made me a couple of gallons of her mama's chicken soup. If the pills don't cure me, you can bet her home cookin' will."

"Well, please, take care of yourself." Phoebe combed trembling fingers through her hair. She shifted her weight from one foot to the other and back again. Swallowing hard, she finally said, "Fridge, if you... if you should hear from Jackson..."

"I'll let you know, Phoebe" came the quick, unequivocal pledge.

Exhaustion enveloped Phoebe as soon as she clicked off the portable phone and set it down. She knew it was pointless to go back to bed. Until she found out where Jackson was and whether he was all right, she wouldn't be able to sleep.

She closed her eyes for a moment.

He'd found a dead child. A little girl. He'd brought her body out of a burning building, probably risking his life in the process.

No matter that the young victim had been a stranger.

No matter that he'd undoubtedly done all that could have been done to save her.

Phoebe could imagine what Jackson must be thinking.
What he must be feeling. She, too, had experienced the bit-
terness of professional "failure."

The grief...

The guilt...

The sound of a car engine made Phoebe open her eyes.
She ran to the living-room window, parting the curtains and
looking outside just in time to see a station wagon pull into
the driveway across the street.

She slumped, her fingers going slack. The draperies
swung closed once again.

After a few moments, Phoebe left the living room and
went into the bathroom. She scrubbed her teeth and
splashed cold water on her face. The reflection she saw in
the mirror hanging over the sink was less than reassuring.
Her complexion was pasty. There were shadows beneath her
eyes.

Fridge Randall had sounded worried, she thought,
gnawing her lower lip. Really, truly worried.

He'd believed Jackson might come to him for succor. And
if not to him, then to her.

But what if...

Oh, God, what if...

A faint rumble caught Phoebe's attention. She stiffened,
cocking her head, scarcely daring to breathe.

Jackson's pickup!

It had to be. It just had to be.

The robe that matched the apricot silk nightgown she was
wearing was hanging on a hook on the back of the bathroom door. She snatched it down and donned it as she
dashed for the living room.

She didn't bother to look out the window. She simply
undid the various safety locks on the front door, flung it
open and walked out into the sunshine of a heartbreakingly
beautiful August morning.

Jackson was approaching the steps that led up to the front
porch. His usually swift and decisive stride had been replaced by a heavy-footed plod. His tawny-haired head was
bowed, his hands were jammed deep into the pockets of his

uniform's ink-blue trousers. The set of his broad shoulders suggested he was braced for a blow.

"Jackson?" Phoebe questioned tentatively. She felt a bead of perspiration trickle down her spine and settle in the small of her back.

Jackson came to an abrupt halt, every line of his body going rigid. After a second or two, he lifted his head.

Phoebe caught her breath, struggling to hide her shock at his appearance. He looked shattered. His skin was stretched taut over the angular bones of his face. His lips were pressed into a thin, bloodless line.

And his eyes. Dear Lord, *his eyes!* They were as lifeless as lead, their vitality drained away, their sky-bright vibrancy extinguished.

"I'm cold, Phoebe," he told her, his voice as empty as his expression. "I'm so damned cold."

An emotion too powerful to be denied prompted Phoebe to extend her hands to him. "Come inside with me," she invited quietly. "I'll help you get warm."

Eight

Jackson was never able to pinpoint the exact moment when the overwhelming chill of loss gave way to the irresistible heat of life. He only knew that such a moment occurred and altered his existence forever.

But before it did, he poured out the story of the death of a twenty-month-old girl who had shared his daughter's fair coloring and his late wife's first name. He sat on Phoebe's sofa—hands fisted, gaze fixed—and talked about the incident until his voice was nearly gone and the ice that had entered his soul when he'd found little Anne had begun to crack.

The length of the silence that fell once he finally stopped speaking wasn't measurable by any traditional standard. But it was sufficient to give him time to recall some of the things he'd said during his angry, anguished monologue. It also offered him plenty of opportunity to reconsider the woman to whom he'd said them.

With that reconsideration came remembrance.

Of an erotic dream ...

Of an incendiary kiss...

Of an inexplicable, first-sight feeling of predestination...

"Come inside with me," she'd urged, her voice soft, her hands outstretched and steady. *"I'll help you get warm."*

Jackson shifted his weight abruptly, conscious of a sudden stirring in his groin. He looked at Phoebe, who was seated in an armchair to his left. Her head was slightly bowed, her face obscured by a glossy curtain of hair. While her posture suggested pensiveness, the way she was twisting the belt of her robe hinted at a more turbulent mood.

Jackson cleared his throat. He watched Phoebe's fine-boned hands still, her silk-wrapped body stiffen. After a moment, she lifted her head and met his gaze. There was a suspicious sheen in her verdant eyes.

Jackson cleared his throat a second time, struggling to absorb the implications of what he was seeing. Not once during his recitation had Phoebe given any sign that she was being upset by what he was telling her. Indeed, it had been her seeming serenity that had given him the strength to say so much.

Did her training—or temperament—enable her to mask her feelings *that* effectively? he wondered uneasily. Had she retreated behind a barrier of professional detachment while he'd dropped his guard and spilled his guts? Had she been treating him the way she would treat a *patient?*

Or had he been so caught up in his own emotional turmoil, so desperate to vent his pain, that he'd been prepared to accept her apparent tranquillity at face value? If he'd taken the time to look—to really look—would he have seen the true impact his words were having on her?

"I'm sorry, Phoebe," he apologized. His voice sounded strange to him. It was rough and raw, as though he'd been sucking in smoke.

"Sorry?" She blinked. "For what?"

He gestured. "For barging in and dumping all this on you. I had no right—"

"You had every right," she interrupted. "I *asked* you in, Jackson. I *asked* you to tell me what happened. There's no need for an apology."

There was another silence. Five seconds into it, Jackson realized that the tightening in his groin hadn't eased. Precisely the opposite, in fact. Five seconds later, he got up from the sofa and declared, "I think I'd better go."

Phoebe rose to her feet, too. The movement caused the apricot-colored silk of her robe to shimmer and shift. Jackson's awareness of the body beneath the lustrous fabric increased tenfold in less time than it took him to draw a single breath. While the cut of the floor-length garment was demure, it embraced the supple lines of her figure like a possessive lover.

"You're welcome to stay," she told him, apparently oblivious to the effect she was having on him. "If you're willing to risk my cooking, I could make you some breakfast. Heaven knows, I owe you about a dozen meals."

"No." Jackson shook his head. "That's okay."

She frowned. "You're sure?"

"Positive." He took a step forward. The move was a mistake. Her scent—a provocative combination of wildflower purity and womanly promise—suddenly insinuated itself into his consciousness. He inhaled deeply, his blood starting to thrum, his body beginning to throb. "You've done more than enough for me."

It was true. Phoebe had done more than enough for him. The problem was, more than enough wasn't all he needed right now and he knew it. He had to get out before he acted on this knowledge . . . or out of that need.

Phoebe raised her chin a notch. She gazed up at him for several seconds. Then her expression began to change. Her nostrils flared. Her eyes flashed and her pupils dilated. The tip of her tongue stole out and curled daintily across her upper lip. Jackson felt the muscles of his belly clench.

Unable to stop himself, he closed the distance between them, then lifted his hands and cupped Phoebe's face. He felt a tremor of reaction run through her. After a few seconds he gently slid his fingers up and back, weaving them through the red-gold tumble of her hair.

She quivered as he traced the sensitive curves of her ears and the softness of their lobes. Her head tilted back slightly, her gilt-lashed eyelids fluttered down.

Jackson mapped the delicate yet decisive shape of her jaw, then molded the elegant line of her slender neck with his palms. His thumbs settled into the faintly shadowed hollow at the base of her throat. The sudden speed-up of her pulse was unmistakable.

"Phoebe," he whispered on a harsh exhalation, acutely conscious of his own accelerating heartbeat. "Oh, darlin'..."

She lured him like a lighted candle might lure a homeless wanderer on a frigid winter night. He knew, of course, that even the smallest flame could be dangerous. Yet every instinct Jackson had told him that the fire he sensed burning within Phoebe Irene Donovan had been kindled to heal, not hurt.

"Come inside with me," she'd said. *"I'll help you get warm."*

Phoebe opened her mouth as though preparing to speak. Jackson bent his head and captured her lips, silencing her before she could utter a single word. Her breath rushed out and blended with his. A moment later, he gathered her into his arms.

Had Phoebe resisted, he would have released her. Or so Jackson reassured himself afterward. Yet he could never completely convince himself this was true. The passion that ignited within him the instant his mouth closed over hers was like nothing he'd ever known.

But Phoebe didn't resist. There was a split second of something—a sort of shocked stillness—then she seemed to melt against him, her body fitting to his as though it had been created for just that purpose. Her lips parted beneath his. The taste of her flooded his consciousness like molten honey.

Jackson fueled the explosive eroticism of the kiss with teeth and tongue. His hands slid down Phoebe's back, clasping her, coaxing her nearer. She shifted sinuously, the movement of her hips both primitive and provocative. He felt his body harden in a sexual reflex that was as basic to human life as DNA.

A few white-hot moments later, Jackson swept Phoebe up and carried her into her bedroom. Moments after that, they were both naked. Who undressed whom was never very clear to him. Had Jackson been told that their garments had been burned away by spontaneous combustion, he would have considered the explanation plausible. What was happening between them was that sudden, that searing.

Phoebe's bared breasts were small and beautifully shaped. Her nipples were taut with yearning. Theirs was an invitation Jackson could not resist. He stroked the burgeoning peaks with his fingers. The plush velvet of her rose-peach aureolas turned to pebbled satin in response to his ministrations.

Dipping his head, Jackson touched the tip of one of Phoebe's breasts with his tongue. The nipple tightened as his lips circled it. She arched, invoking his name on a broken breath, as he took the pouting bud of flesh deep into his mouth.

Swaying like a reed in a strong wind, Phoebe clutched at his shoulders. Her slender fingers spasmed in counterpoint to his rhythmic sucking. Her nails scored his skin.

Eventually Jackson kissed his way back to her mouth and claimed the sweet heat of her lips once again. He felt her hands straying restlessly over his flesh, scorching him to the bone.

"Phoebe," he groaned. "Oh, God. Phoebe."

They went down on her unmade bed together, their limbs tangling amid the sleep-tumbled linens. Jackson caressed Phoebe more and more intimately.

The cluster of fiery curls at the apex of her smooth-skinned thighs was soft. The layered flesh hidden beneath the triangle of red-gold hair was softer still. Jackson traced the petal-like folds with infinite gentleness, seeking and finding the core of Phoebe's responsiveness. She shuddered and gave a wild little cry as he touched the nerve-rich nubbin of flesh. The sound she made sizzled through his nervous system like a bolt of lightning. The tips of his fingers grew slick with the dew of her arousal.

"Please." Phoebe's voice was husky. Her pupils had grown so huge that a narrow rim of jade green was all that remained of her irises. Her body curved into his. "Please, Jackson."

His desire for her was elemental. Absolute. It went beyond anything he'd ever experienced or dreamed. He needed her the way he needed air to breathe and water to drink. She seemed the essence of life itself.

With a throttled groan, Jackson shifted his position, then sheathed himself within the welcoming warmth of Phoebe's body. The gliding, sliding shock of the first full moment of their joining nearly undid him. He went rigid, trying to hold himself in check.

"Don't—" he gulped for air "—move."

"I..." she shook her head, her delicate features contorting "...c-can't..."

"*You can.*"

A few more seconds. That's all he was asking. Just a few more seconds...

A wave of heat surged through him. Jackson started to shake like a man in the grip of a raging fever. His body and brain were on fire.

And then he sensed the first tiny ripples of Phoebe's release. Her body tightened, her flesh caressing his with indescribable intimacy.

Jackson began to thrust. Deep. Then deeper still. Phoebe arched upward, his name breaking from her lips on a ragged sob.

"Phoe—" Jackson's voice shattered along with his control. The second syllable he was trying to say wedged in his throat. His breath seemed to dam up behind it. He thrust one more time. "—be!"

The world went up in flames.

Jackson burned... and felt reborn.

What have I done?

Phoebe had been asking herself this question for the better part of an hour.

The first time she'd asked it, she'd been lying in the circle of Jackson's strong arms. She'd been wide-awake, her body reverberating with the aftermath of ecstasy, her brain reeling with the implications of what had occurred. Her partner in passion, on the other hand, had been fast asleep. His heartbeat had been slow and steady, his breathing deep and even. He'd seemed like a man at peace with himself and the world around him.

Jackson had gathered her close before he'd drifted off, stroking her body with long, languid caresses. He'd also nuzzled at her hair and murmured something deep in his throat. Exactly what this "something" had been, Phoebe wasn't certain. That it hadn't been "What have I done?" she was absolutely sure.

She'd lain next to Jackson for several increasingly frustrated minutes before easing herself out of his embrace and getting up. He'd rolled over onto his back almost as soon as she'd vacated the bed, flinging his arms wide and staking a claim on ninety percent of the mattress. He'd also spoken again. A single word this time, articulated very clearly.

"Phoebe," he'd said.

The sound of her name on his lips had sent a shiver of pleasure coursing through her. She'd crossed her arms in front of her bare breasts and bitten the inside of her cheek, trying to steel herself against the involuntary response.

What have I done? she'd asked herself again.

She'd stood by the bed, gazing down at Jackson for a long time. The urge to reach out and touch him—to trace the strong arch of his brows, the slightly crooked line of his nose, the sensuous curve of his lower lip—had been very strong. Yet she'd forced herself to resist it. Eventually she'd forced herself to turn away.

Feeling curiously like an intruder, she'd moved around her bedroom, picking up the garments she and Jackson had left strewn around the floor. The memory of how they'd gotten from fully dressed to totally naked had flowed through her mind in an incandescent blur as she'd gone about the tidying up process.

Again and again, she'd glanced toward the tawny-haired man who lay sleeping in her bed. Again and again, she'd asked herself the question: *What have I done?*

She'd found some clothes—cotton briefs, jeans and a loose-fitting T-shirt—and put them on. Then she'd gathered her tangled hair back into a haphazard ponytail and secured it with a rubber band. Finally she'd tiptoed out of the bedroom. Her heart had been beating much more rapidly than normal and her breath had been coming in shallow little pants. She'd been acutely conscious of the way the denim of her jeans rubbed against the skin of her inner thighs.

She was *still* conscious of it. Every time she moved, every time she shifted her weight, Phoebe felt the friction of stiff fabric against soft flesh. While the sensation was not unpleasant, her awareness of it was unnerving. Because with that awareness came the memory of Jackson's hard palms moving up her legs, of his lean fingers gleaning her body's most sensitive secrets, of his warm breath fanning her trembling lips a split second before he—

"Stop it!" Phoebe ordered herself, dropping down onto the sofa she'd bolted from barely two minutes ago. Leaning forward, she braced her elbows on her knees and buried her face in her upturned palms. She drew a shuddery breath, trying to ignore the seductive tendrils of heat that were uncoiling deep within her.

Dear God, she thought, pressing her cheeks against the heels of her hands. *What have I done?*

She answered the question as she'd answered it the first time she'd asked it and every time since.

What she'd done was fall in love with Jackson Stuart Miller.

What have I done?

The question condensed inside Jackson's slumber-clouded brain along with the hazy realization that the bed in which he was so comfortably sprawled was not his own.

Details about his situation began to seep into his consciousness.

He was alone in the bed that was not his own.

He was alone . . . and he was lying naked amid a tangle of pastel sheets. These sheets carried the musky scent of sex and male sweat as well as the wildflower fragrance of a woman's—

Comprehension jolted Jackson like an electric shock. Every fiber of his body and brain switched from half awake to fully alert. He sat bolt upright, the sluice gates of his mind opening, the memories pouring in.

"I'm cold," he'd said, remembering the sight of a dead child's cornsilk-fair hair, the sound of her mother wailing her name over and over. *"I'm so damned cold."*

"Come inside with me," Phoebe had responded, holding out her hands to him. *"I'll help you get warm."*

Had she really meant—?

More to the point, had it really mattered to him?

Jackson squeezed his eyes shut.

God. When he thought about the way he'd behaved! He'd always prided himself on his self-control, on putting his partner's pleasure before his own. Yet with Phoebe he'd been quick and careless, like some selfish would-be stud. He'd been driven, almost desperate. He'd forced the pace. Forced the passion.

Perhaps he'd even forced her?

Jackson's throat closed up, his stomach roiled. He clenched his hands. No, he denied, shaking his head. Merciful heaven, no. He couldn't have. He *wouldn't* have!

And yet . . .

Jackson opened his eyes, then flung back the sheets and got to his feet. His clothes were draped neatly over the end of the bed. He reached for his trousers.

What have I done? he demanded of himself as he zipped and buttoned his fly.

He couldn't answer the question. But he knew, for better or worse, that Phoebe Irene Donovan could.

What he didn't know was whether she would . . . or how he'd react if she did.

* * *

Phoebe had just clicked off the cordless phone when

Jackson walked into the living room. Although she had her back to the door and his entrance was noiseless, she sensed his presence immediately. The rush of awareness gave her a moment to prepare herself before she turned to face him. Heaven knew, she needed it!

Jackson had come to a halt six or seven feet away from her. He was too far away to hear the sudden thudding of her heart, something for which she was deeply grateful. He was also too far away to touch her. Her feelings about this circumstance vacillated between relief and regret.

The shattered look he'd worn earlier was gone. In its place was a calmly disciplined expression. The light was back in his eyes as well, although she thought she glimpsed a certain wariness flickering through their indigo depths.

Jackson was himself again, Phoebe decided after a moment.

Or was he?

The longer she gazed at him, the increasingly different Jackson seemed to be. Then again, perhaps she was simply assessing him in a new way. While she'd never subscribed to the old adage about love being blind, Phoebe did believe that love was capable of irreparably altering a person's perception of the world.

Maybe it had something to do with his ruffled hair and rumpled clothing. Or with the uncharacteristically awkward way he kept shifting his weight back and forth between his bare feet. But there was an aura of uncertainty— no, an aura of *vulnerability* about Jackson. It was a quality she'd never detected in him before.

He'd been vulnerable earlier, of course. Vulnerable in the sense that he'd broken, briefly, under a burden of grief and guilt that he'd taken it upon himself to shoulder. But the vulnerability Phoebe felt emanating from him now was... was...well, for all her psychiatric expertise, the only way she could describe it was as *different*.

"Hi," she said finally.

"Hi," he replied.

"I was talking to Fridge." She gestured with the telephone. "He called earlier. He'd heard about what happened at the fire."

Jackson didn't appear surprised by this information. "From Keezia."

"Yes." Phoebe set the instrument down. "She phoned him after she saw you at the station. He thought you might drop by to visit him. But when you didn't, he, uh, uh—"

"Figured I'd come to you." While the comment was quiet, the intensity with which it was uttered made Phoebe's pulse quicken.

"He was worried," she amended, fiddling with the hem of the cotton top she was wearing. She could feel her nipples pressing against the soft fabric of the garment and wished desperately that she'd taken the time to don a bra before she'd snuck out of her bedroom. "I promised I'd let him know if—when—you got home. I told him you were all right." She hesitated, trying to read Jackson's expression. After a few moments, she came to the conclusion that she'd have more luck deciphering hieroglyphics without the aid of the Rosetta stone. She took a step forward and asked, "You *are* all right, aren't you?"

"I'm better than I was." He studied her with disconcerting directness for several seconds. His gaze flicked down for a moment, then returned to her face. "What about you?"

"Me? What about . . . me?"

Jackson moved, lessening the distance that separated them by a long, lithe stride. "Are *you* all right?"

She blinked, taken aback by the abrupt turning of the conversational tables. Did Jackson suspect? she wondered. Had she somehow betrayed the feelings she'd discovered as she'd lain in his arms?

"Phoebe?"

"I'm fine," she said quickly, summoning up a smile to support the lie. "Just fine."

Jackson took another step toward her. Phoebe couldn't help noticing that his posture had suddenly become very rigid. The set of his shoulders was stiff beneath his partially buttoned shirt. His arms were locked at his sides, hands fisted against his thighs. It was almost as though he feared the consequences of coming too close to her. But why in the name of heaven . . . ?

"I didn't—" he paused, seeming to struggle with his choice of words "—hurt you?"

The shock Phoebe felt at this inquiry was too profound for her to disguise. "Y-you?" she stammered. "Hurt . . . m-me?"

"Did I?" The question was short and sharp.

"No!" She shook her head, causing her ponytailed hair to bounce back and forth between her shoulder blades. "How can you possibly—"

"How can I possibly not?" Jackson countered, his blue eyes bright with self-directed anger. "I didn't ask you to make love with me, Phoebe. I never gave you an opportunity to say 'yes' or 'no' or 'maybe some other time.' I was so caught up in my own wants, my own needs, that I just did it! And I didn't even think to take care of you while I did!"

Phoebe stared at him, stunned. Her mind replayed his last sentence several times. He hadn't "taken care" of her? What was he trying to say? That he believed he'd failed to satisfy her in bed?

No, she thought. There was no way in the world Jackson couldn't know the effect he'd had on her. Given the cries she'd made at the peak of their passion, the scratches she'd inflicted on his back when she'd clung to him as she'd broken apart with pleasure—he *had* to know!

"Jackson," she began throatily, "if you'd 'taken care' of me any more than you did, I'd be scattered all over the bedroom in a million pieces right now."

It was the frankest acknowledgment of a sexual response Phoebe had ever made. Nonetheless, she knew it erred on the side of understatement. What she'd experienced with Jackson was beyond her ability to describe.

Describing her lover's reaction to her uncharacteristically bold statement of fact was no easily accomplished task, either. At first, Jackson looked blank, as though her words hadn't registered. Then he flushed. Phoebe watched a series of emotions sleet across his compelling features. He seemed utterly flabbergasted one instant, immensely flattered the next.

Finally Jackson cleared his throat. The color in his lean cheeks was still much higher than usual. "I was talking about the fact that I didn't use any protection with you," he clarified softly.

Phoebe gulped, feeling the bones in her legs start to liquify. She decided it was time to sit down. The armchair she'd used earlier was a few steps away. Somehow, she managed to navigate the distance and seat herself. She lowered her gaze to the floor. She was trembling.

"Phoebe?"

She allowed herself a moment to compose herself, then looked up. She experienced an odd little thrill when she saw that Jackson had moved to within touching distance.

"I'm on the Pill," she said, forcing herself to meet his eyes squarely. "So you don't need to worry about birth control. As for other concerns ... I underwent a complete physical when I joined the hospital staff, four months ago. I got a clean bill of health. You—" she swallowed hard "—you're the first man I've been intimate with since then."

In point of fact, Jackson Stuart Miller was the first man Phoebe had been intimate with since her fiancé's death. But she wasn't ready to admit that. Not now. Probably not later, either.

"I donated blood a couple of weeks ago," Jackson responded, giving no clue as to his reaction to her last sentence. "AB positive. No nasty viruses."

Phoebe let a few seconds of silence tick by, then chided herself for doing so. What was she waiting for? she demanded of herself. A summary of Jackson's sexual history? That the man was an experienced lover had been abundantly obvious to her. Did she really want to hear about the women with whom he'd gained his erotic expertise?

No, of course she didn't want to hear about them. She didn't even want to think about them!

Phoebe inhaled on a shaky breath, then expelled it on a carefully controlled sigh. "Well, then," she finally said. "Everything's ... okay."

"Is it?"

There was a challenging edge to the question. Phoebe drew herself up and cocked her chin. "Yes."

"You don't think we need to talk about what happened between us?"

"Isn't that what we've been doing?"

Jackson narrowed his eyes and folded his arms across his chest. "Are you suggesting we've exhausted the subject?"

"I'm suggesting we need to keep the subject in perspective."

"Meaning?"

"Meaning, you had an understandable reaction to a tragic set of circumstances. The way you were when you got home—" Phoebe broke off, appalled by a sudden change in Jackson's expression. He looked like a man who'd taken a mortal blow.

"You went to bed with me out of pity?"

"No!" The denial was as spontaneous as it was sincere. Quite a contrast to her exquisitely careful phrasings of the past few minutes. "No, of course not!"

Suddenly Jackson was looming over her, his hands gripping the arms of the chair where she was seated, effectively trapping her in place. "Then what *did* you feel for me when we made love, Phoebe?" he demanded, his features taut, his voice harsh. "And what the hell do you feel for me now?"

She almost told him. Almost, but not quite. Nor did she fling the question back at him as she desperately longed to do.

"I ... care ... about you," she said after a few seconds, fighting to keep her voice steady. "What happened between us—our making love together—it was a natural thing. Don't you see, Jackson? The desire to affirm life in the face of death is a very potent human impulse. It's a way of coping. This morning, after the fire, you *needed* someone!"

Jackson stopped her by the simple expedient of pressing the fingers of his right hand against her mouth. The tenderness of the gesture made her quiver clear down to her toes.

"No," he contradicted. The tightness was gone from his face, the harshness from his tone. "I needed *you*, Phoebe. I wanted *you*. Not...someone. *You*."

Phoebe stared into his eyes. They'd gone very dark. They looked deep enough to drown in.

"But the needing and the wanting didn't start this morning," Jackson went on, his fingers drifting slowly down the line of her throat. "Because when it comes to potent human impulses..." He shook his head. "I can't tell you I've been celibate for the past four months, darlin'. But I haven't so much as looked at another woman since the night you fell into my arms."

His name escaped her lips on a rush of breath.

"You felt it from the beginning, too, didn't you?" he asked, reversing the direction of his caress. "And you feel it now."

Phoebe averted her face slightly. She had to. She was afraid of what Jackson might read in her eyes if she didn't.

Yes, she felt it. The hot, honeyed awareness. The slow, sensual melting. The needing. The wanting. And more. So much more, she ached with it.

After a few moments, she forced herself to meet Jackson's gaze once again. "I thought you thought being involved with me would get complicated," she said, echoing the statement Lauralee had made to her between bites of peach pie more than a month ago.

Jackson stiffened for an instant, his hand stilling. Then he obviously deduced the source of her information. His body relaxed. "I think I thought right," he answered with a hint of rueful humor. "But since one of the complicating factors is gone until Labor Day..."

Phoebe licked her lips. She saw desire streak through the depths of Jackson's eyes like a lightning bolt. A tremor skittered up her spine.

"I don't...I don't know if I'm ready for this, Jackson," she finally said. It was the truth. Not the whole truth, to be sure. But a portion of it.

"I don't know if I'm ready for this, either," he answered, the left corner of his mouth curling up. The dimple on that side of his face indented for just an instant. "Whatever 'this' is. But I'd like to find out. The thing is, there's only one way for me to do it, and that's with you."

Jackson straightened as he spoke the last four words, then took a step back. He stood there, gazing down at Phoebe for several long, silent seconds. Finally he held out his hands to her.

Phoebe hesitated, torn as she had never been torn in her life. She loved him. She *loved* Jackson Stuart Miller. Yet she understood what he was. What he did for a living. She knew the chances he took and the risks he ran. Dear Lord, if anything were to happen to him . . .

"Don't be afraid, Phoebe," he counseled softly.

But she was. She was absolutely terrified. Still, despite her fear, Phoebe found it impossible not to reach for what was being offered.

Palms slid over palms. A moment later, Jackson's strong fingers curled around Phoebe's slender wrists. A moment after that, he pulled her to her feet and into an embrace. She turned her face up toward his.

"Darlin'," he murmured huskily. "Oh, darlin' . . ."

Then he dipped his head and kissed her.

Where the movements of his mouth over hers had once been frantic and fevered, they were now slow and seductive. He courted and coaxed, never pressing a claim until Phoebe was eager to surrender all he wanted and more.

"J-Jackson," she whispered shakily when the kiss finally came to an end. "Oh, Jackson . . ."

She lifted her right hand and stroked the left side of his face. A faint bristling of new beard growth sandpapered the smooth skin of her palm. After a second or two, she touched the center of his firm, flexible lips. They parted. She felt the misty puff of his breath against her fingertips followed by the teasing lick of his tongue.

Jackson gathered Phoebe close, making her dizzyingly aware of the potent thrust of his arousal. He sculpted the sleek line of her thighs and womanly swell of her hips. His fingers flexed once, as though he wanted to test the resilience of feminine flesh beneath the denim jeans. Then he stroked upward, his hands slipping beneath the loose-fitting pullover she had on.

Phoebe was trembling with anticipation by the time he finally caressed his way to her breasts. He cupped them gently, molding their shape with his palms. He feathered the work-hardened pads of his thumbs against the sensitive inner curves of her cleavage, moving outward toward her nipples in tiny, torturous increments.

She cried out when Jackson finally touched the aching, passion-engorged peaks. The sensation that arrowed through her in the first instant of contact was so intense it was almost agony.

They kissed again. Deeply. Demandingly. Phoebe slid her hands down from her lover's broad, suavely muscled shoulders and undid the buttons of his shirt. Parting the garment with an impatient gesture, she began winnowing her fingers through the rough silk of his chest hair. Jackson made a guttural sound when she found the furled buds of flesh that she was seeking and raked them lightly with her nails.

More kisses. More caresses.

Jackson's ink-blue shirt fluttered to the floor. A heartbeat or two later, Phoebe's cotton top followed. The rubber band that had been holding her ponytail snapped as the garment was pulled over her head. Her hair spilled free around her face and over her newly bared shoulders.

"Lovely," Jackson said hoarsely. "You are so...lovely."

Then, with the ineffable male grace that was so much a part of him, he sank onto his knees in front of her.

Dazed—almost drugged—with emotion, it took Phoebe a few seconds to comprehend Jackson's intentions. By the time she did, he'd undone her jeans and peeled them, plus the plain cotton panties underneath, down her legs.

As a thirty-four-year-old psychiatrist, Phoebe Irene Donovan was neither innocent nor ignorant. But her personal sexual experience was limited. She'd never...ever...

Jackson's hands glided up from the backs of her knees. She felt his fingers splay and curve, conforming to the shape of her buttocks. After a moment, his hold on her tightened. He drew her toward him.

"Jack-son..." she whimpered.

He pressed his lips against her belly, his tongue dipping into the shallow indentation of her navel. Muscles deep within Phoebe's body contracted in response. They released in a fluttering rush a second later as Jackson began to kiss his way down to the red-gold curls that clustered between her thighs.

"*Jackson,*" she repeated.

He lifted his head. "Let me, darlin'," he said hoarsely. "Please. Let me do this for you."

Phoebe closed her eyes and did as she'd been bidden.

The warmth of his breath against the skin of her inner thighs...

The nuzzle of his mouth against the delta-shaped badge of her sex...

The languid lap of his tongue...

Phoebe gasped. Then gasped again, her body arching in instinctive, unstoppable reaction.

Jackson pleasured her with unstinting generosity. His touch was infinitely skilled, his timing impeccable. He seemed able to gauge her capacity for erotic response to the nth degree.

But pleasure unshared ultimately became unsatisfying, then empty. Phoebe opened her eyes. Reaching down, she tangled her fingers in Jackson's tawny hair and tugged.

He looked up at her once again. His lean-featured face was flushed. His blue eyes blazed with the same brilliance they'd held in her dream.

"Be with me," Phoebe whispered. "Be with me."

Slowly Jackson got to his feet. He staggered a little, not quite centered. Then, catlike, he recovered his balance. "Phoebe—"

Her jeans and panties had puddled around her feet. Phoebe stepped out of the pool of clothing and kicked it away. "*Please.*"

She did not have to repeat her plea.

Somehow, they made it over to the sofa. Somehow, Jackson managed to unsnap, unzip and shuck his trousers. The sight of his rampant masculinity sent a very feminine thrill running through Phoebe. She reached out for him. He moved to her.

They sprawled on the cushions of the couch, mouths mated, bodies locked heart to heart.

"Darlin'..." Jackson breathed, kissing a burning path from her lips to her throat. He nuzzled at her hair and nipped at her earlobe. "Oh, sweet darlin'..."

Phoebe felt the nudge of his knee between her thighs. She opened to him instantly. Wanting him. Needing him. Loving him.

"Now," she urged.

Jackson entered her, sliding inside her body as though he belonged there. Possessing, yet being possessed in turn. Phoebe lifted her hips at the same instant he began to thrust. Which one of them set the rhythm for what followed mattered not at all. Their movements were utterly, absolutely attuned.

"Phoebe," he groaned.

To know the heat of him. And the hardness. To hear the rasping pant of his breath and the pounding beat of his hammering heart. To understand that *she* had brought him to this state.

Lord, it was almost more than she could bear!

"Jackson." She gazed up into his lean, perspiration-sheened face. His passion-hazed eyes were sultry beneath heavy, half-lowered lids. "Oh, Jackson."

They reached the pinnacle together. Phoebe felt the first pulse of his release a split second after her own body began to spasm with a fierce, flooding ecstasy.

It was consummation.

It was completion.

It was an act of courage, compelled by love.

Nine

During the days that followed, there were a number of moments when Phoebe came very close to sharing her fears with Jackson. But she could never quite find the right way to articulate her emotions.

She was honest enough to admit that one of the reasons for her reluctance to speak was the recognition that she couldn't simply say, "Jackson, you have a dangerous job and I'm frightened for you." She knew she'd have to tell him that she was frightened for herself, as well.

She was frightened of loving him the way she did.

Even worse, she was frightened of *losing* him the way she'd lost her father and her fiancé.

How would Jackson Stuart Miller—a fifth-generation firefighter, a man for whom courage was a family tradition—react if she confessed to harboring such fears?

Phoebe didn't know, which was another reason she kept silent. It seemed to her that the women Jackson held nearest and dearest—his late wife, his daughter and his mother—had always supported him in his chosen career. If she, a

woman with no permanent place in h
questioning his job...

Love the man, she thought. Love his wo

Or, at the very least, try to make peace w

"Any professional tips about how to put
on?"

"One leg at a time, darlin'. The same way you
off."

Phoebe slanted a sharp look at her lover of less
week. "You're *so* helpful, Lieutenant Miller."

"I strive to please, Dr. Donovan" came the drawlin
ply.

The time was a few minutes after eight in the evening
the second Friday in August. The setting was the one-story
brick firehouse where Jackson, Fridge Randall and the ten
other members of the station's A-shift crew had already
clocked more than thirteen hours of duty. Phoebe, who'd
put in ten-hours-plus at her own job, was about to cap a tour
of the facility by trying on a full set of turnout gear.

The scene was not the one she'd envisioned that morning
when she'd broached the possibility of her paying a visit to
the station. She'd raised the matter casually, over breakfast, without any firm itinerary in mind.

Jackson's initial reaction to her suggestion had been surprise—astonishment, even. But once he'd accepted that her
request was sincere, he'd proposed she stop by the firehouse on her way home from the hospital.

"You mean, tonight?" she'd asked, conscious of a sudden prickling of uneasiness.

"Sure," he'd affirmed, getting up from the kitchen table. "It's my turn to cook for the crew. What do you say?"

She'd said the only thing she could, given the circumstances.

"Great," he'd responded, moving around to where she
was seated. She'd turned her face up and he'd given her a
quick kiss. "I'll feed you a decent dinner, then take you
around the station."

his word. After producing a
best versions of jambalaya
isted Fridge's help in giv-
se. Their running com-
tag-team storytelling
d Muster.
sked at one point,
everything she was
pment would be impec-
prised her. That its floors
to eat off of had.
ridge had answered.
he broom-and-bucket routine right af-
uster," Jackson had elaborated.
firefighters have to do *housework?*"
uh."

ackson was a regular johnny-moppin' genius before he
ot enough seniority to stop squattin' in front of bathroom
bowls," Fridge had remarked with a molasses-rich chuckle.
"I've never met another white boy with so much natural
talent for scrubbin' toilets."

Phoebe had glanced back and forth between the two men,
uncertain whether she was being teased. "Really?"

"Really." Jackson had grinned, clearly amused by her
reaction. "I used to wash windows, too. Firefighters are re-
sponsible for the upkeep of their stations, inside and out."

She'd shaken her head. "I had no idea."

"Most civilians don't."

Jackson's comment had been offhanded—the verbal
equivalent of a shrug of resignation. Yet it had stung
Phoebe. She'd experienced a sudden resurgence of the sense
of being stuck on the outside peering in that she'd felt so
frequently during her adolescence.

A few minutes later, Jackson had asked whether she
wanted to "get a feel" for some real firefighting gear. Her
answer had been an unequivocal affirmative.

Then she'd seen the amount of equipment she'd so enthusiastically agreed to put on.

"While Lieutenant Miller is strivin' to please, let me succeed at providin' you with some assistance in getting into those pants, Phoebe," Fridge offered, extending his right hand with a gallant flourish.

"Thanks." Phoebe grasped the black firefighter's callused palm and used it to steady herself as she stepped into the garment Jackson was holding open for her.

The "pants" combined protective leggings with thick-soled boots and came equipped with a pair of wide leather suspenders. Jackson pulled these up Phoebe's arms and over her shoulders. By the time he was finished adjusting them to his satisfaction, she was tingling clear down to her heavily shod toes.

Phoebe drew a steadying breath. "Now what?" she asked, trying to ignore the heat licking through her veins.

"Turnout coat."

Phoebe donned the thigh-length garment and, after some fumbling, fastened its various snaps, flaps and hooks. The bulkiness of the garment reminded her of the quilted snowsuits she'd been bundled into as a child in Boston.

"Gloves next," Fridge said, bringing out a pair of reinforced gauntlets. Phoebe pulled them on, too. She flexed her fingers experimentally, noting that the gloves didn't have much give.

"Do you want to try the breathing apparatus?" Jackson queried, hefting a metal tank that looked a lot like something a scuba diver might use.

"Ah, sure."

The tank was strapped into place in a matter of seconds. Phoebe rotated her shoulders, trying to accustom herself to the additional burden. How in heaven's name did firefighters do their jobs wearing all this gear? she wondered. The equipment she was wearing had to weigh sixty, maybe seventy, pounds. She could only imagine what it must be like to run around in it on a sizzling summer day.

"How much air is there in this tank?" she asked.

"About a half hour's worth, if you breathe normally."

Phoebe adjusted her stance, not wanting to speculate about what would be considered "normal" breathing inside a burning building. "How do you know when you're running out?"

"There's a timer." Jackson gestured for her to turn around. She pivoted clumsily, then felt him fiddling with the tank on her back. After a second or two, she heard a short, sharp *ding!* "When that goes off," he said as she turned back to face him, "you get out."

"Thirty minutes is pretty much all a person can take inside a workin' fire," Fridge verified. "Forget those movies where you see the firefighters goin' nonstop in some towerin' inferno for hours 'n' hours. It doesn't happen that way. The other thing the movies get wrong is showin' firefighters chargin' around without masks." He glanced at Jackson. "I guess they figure it makes 'em look extra heroic."

"There was a time when wearing a mask was considered kind of sissy," Jackson commented, fitting the item of equipment under discussion over Phoebe's face. "Nowadays, though, anybody who goes without one is considered stupid."

Phoebe peered at him. "Why the change in attitude?"

"Dirtier smoke."

"Dirtier—?"

"She still needs headgear," Fridge interrupted.

"Got it right here," Jackson responded immediately, producing a helmet and positioning it gently on top of Phoebe's skull. Then he stepped back and assessed her for several seconds. "How do you feel, darlin'?"

Phoebe considered. She'd begun to perspire. Profusely. The mask was chafing her cheeks and forehead. Each time she inhaled, the air tank banged against her spine. She was also aware of several extremely irritating itches—on the tip of her nose, for instance—that she was in no position to scratch.

So, how did she feel?

The phrase "hot and bothered" came to mind.

The firefighter Phoebe loved gave her a knowing smile when she admitted as much.

"Jackson?"

"Mmm?"

"You didn't mind my coming to the fire station yesterday, did you?"

Jackson yawned. "Not at all."

He hoped this response would satisfy Phoebe. One of the things he'd learned about the woman now lying in his arms was that lovemaking seemed to have a loosening effect on her tongue. Unfortunately postcoital communication wasn't something at which he excelled and he knew it. This was not to say that he'd characterize himself as the wham-bam-roll-over-and-start-snoring type. Jackson liked to cuddle. He could usually manage a few after-the-fact compliments for his partners, too. But when it came to participating in a coherent conversation . . .

There was a long pause. Jackson yawned a second time and adjusted his position a bit. Phoebe moved with him, the soft weight of her breasts pressing against his chest. He brushed his lips against her hair, savoring its silken texture and clean scent. A nap, he thought. It was time for a nice, long Saturday afternoon nap.

He inhaled deeply through his nostrils, then exhaled on a slow sigh of satisfaction. A very pleasurable kind of lassitude stole over him. His eyelids grew heavier and heavier. He let them drift shut.

Then Phoebe said, "Jackson?"

Phoebe's previous invocation of his name had been rather dreamy. This time she sounded determined, as though she'd spent the past few moments psyching herself up to speak.

Jackson opened his eyes. "Yeah, darlin'?" he replied with a touch of wariness.

Phoebe lifted her head and looked at him. "Did Anne ever visit you at work?"

Jackson blinked, taken aback by the question. "Uh, sure," he said. "A few times."

Phoebe lowered her lashes. "I see."

She did?

Jackson found himself starting to feel defensive. Easing Phoebe aside, he levered himself into a sitting position, then leaned over and switched on the lamp that sat on the table next to his bed.

"Look, I don't want you to think Anne wasn't interested in my job," he said. "She was. We just tended to, ah, keep things separate."

Phoebe sat up, too, holding the bed sheet against her naked body with one hand and scooping her red-gold tumble of hair back from her face with the other. "Things?"

"What I did at work. What we had together at home."

"She didn't mind?"

"Of course not." The response was automatic. Unthinking. But then something inside Jackson kicked him to reconsider. "She never said anything," he qualified uncomfortably. "But if Anne had wanted me to talk about my job, I would have." He gestured. "I mean, I've certainly talked about it a lot with you."

There was a short silence. Jackson scrutinized Phoebe's expression, trying to figure out where her line of questioning was going. The pensive yet penetrating look in her eyes and the furrow between her brows suggested she was heading down a path he'd prefer not to follow.

Introspection was not—had never been—Jackson's thing. He acted, not analyzed. Yet in recent days, he'd found himself looking inward more and more frequently. What he saw when he did so, he was still a long way from figuring out. And as for whether he *liked* whatever it was he was seeing . . .

"Did your parents tend to keep things separate, too, Jackson?" Phoebe asked suddenly.

"Am I going to get a bill for this session, darlin'?" The counter-query came out a lot sharper than Jackson intended. He experienced a pang of dismay when he saw Phoebe stiffen. Dammit, he hadn't meant— Well, actually, he had. Although he had great respect for Phoebe's profession, he resented the idea that it might influence her personal relationship with him.

In point of fact, his parents had tended to keep things *very* separate. So what? Theirs had been an extremely happy marriage. Would it have been improved if his father had dragged the nitty-gritty reality of his work home with him? No! Of course not.

His father had once told him that he always showered at the end of a shift. "Some things are better left at the station," he'd commented rather cryptically. "A man should be fresh for his family."

It wasn't until after Jackson had joined the fire department that he'd understood what his father had been trying to communicate. And once he'd understood, he, too, had begun showering at the end of each one of his shifts.

He'd forsaken this careful cleansing only once in his fourteen-year career. He'd done so six days ago, on the morning after the night he'd been too late to save a little girl named Anne.

He'd been anything but "fresh" when he'd shown up on Phoebe's doorstep that morning. Even now, the memory of how he'd acted made him want to—

"I'm sorry, Jackson."

Jackson started. For a moment or two, he was unable to comprehend why Phoebe should feel compelled to apologize to him. Then he recalled the comment he'd made and what had prompted it.

Phoebe repeated his name on a questioning inflection. Her eyes were anxious, her mouth tremulous.

Jackson shook his head. "No, darlin'," he disputed quietly, reaching out and gathering her into his arms. "I'm the one who's sorry."

"I know I ask a lot of questions," Phoebe said with a sigh, relaxing into his embrace and nestling against his chest. The soft fan of her breath affected Jackson as if it were a caress. He felt a sudden tightening in his groin. "But I'm trying to understand you. And asking questions is the best way I know to do that."

"I'll take all the understanding I can get, Phoebe." He sifted the fiery strands of her hair through his fingers, weighing the words he wanted—*needed*—to say next. "It's just that, well, there are times when I get the feeling you consider me a candidate for one of those leather couches you psychiatrists supposedly use."

Phoebe's head snapped up. *"Wh-what?"* she stammered, obviously stunned by his admission. "How could you possibly—for heaven's sake, Jackson! You're one of the sanest people I've ever known."

The conviction in her vibrant voice rocked Jackson to the very core of his being. Eventually he sought equilibrium in humor.

"One of the sanest people you've ever known, hmm?" he repeated, striving for a teasing tone. "Even though I make my living running into burning buildings while everybody else is running out?"

Phoebe studied him steadily for several silent seconds. Then she smiled. The slow curving of her lips was lovely to see. Yet when Jackson summoned up the image of it many days later, he realized the expression had never touched her eyes. They'd remained serious. Almost . . . sad.

"Yes," she told him huskily, lifting her arms and twining them around his neck. "As crazy as it sounds, the answer is yes."

Jackson cast a sideward glance at the woman who'd been sharing his bed for ten days and fueling his fantasies for at least as many weeks.

Lord, she looked good!

No matter that her face was bare of makeup and her hair pulled back into a haphazard ponytail. Her allure didn't rely on cosmetic artifice. And when it came to the skimpy white tank top and shortie white shorts she had on . . .

Yes, indeed, Jackson thought. Dr. Phoebe Irene Donovan was appetizing enough to eat. In fact, if he hadn't been on the verge of initiating her into the fine art of frying chicken, he probably would have succumbed to the delectable temptation she offered and started sampling.

A nibble at the back of her neck . . .

A taste of the upper swell of her breasts . . .

Jackson inhaled sharply, dragging his attention back to the task at hand. He gave one last turn to the pepper grinder he was gripping. Considering the skittery jump of his pulse, the steadiness of his fingers was nothing short of remarkable.

"All right," he said, setting the grinder down on the tiled surface of his kitchen counter. "That's one cup of flour plus one and a half teaspoons of salt and two teaspoons of freshly ground pepper."

"Nothing else?" Phoebe leaned in slightly, studying the coating mixture he'd begun sifting together. The subtle floral fragrance of her perfume teased Jackson's nostrils. "You don't put in any special herbs or spices?"

"Not according to my daddy."

"This is his recipe?"

"In a manner of speaking." Jackson finished combining the dry ingredients into a flat baking dish and put the sifter aside. Then he turned toward Phoebe. "It's a family legacy, supposedly handed down from Stuart Nathan Miller himself."

"And you're willing to share it with me?"

"Self-defense, darlin'."

Phoebe cocked her chin. "Is that another reference to my meat loaf, Lieutenant Miller?"

"Oh, is *that* what that was? Meat loaf?"

"Jackson..."

Jackson controlled a grin, flashing back on the events of the previous evening. For reasons she'd only vaguely explained, Phoebe had decided to make dinner for him. To say her efforts had been unsuccessful was to understate the case. Although she'd been upset at first, he'd eventually managed to persuade her that he genuinely didn't give a damn whether or not she could cook. Once she'd accepted that truth, she'd allowed herself to be coaxed into laughter about the situation.

"It wasn't a complete loss," he reminded her. "We found out the smoke detector in your kitchen's working."

Phoebe rolled her eyes. "Oh, right. And I also learned that you're supposed to prick potatoes before you put them into bake."

"Those suckers really blew up, didn't they? I haven't heard that kind of noise since, uh, uh—"

"Since those shotgun shells went off in that house fire four years ago and hit you in the . . . ahem . . . gluteus maximus?" came the dulcet suggestion.

Now Jackson rolled *his* eyes. Although he didn't go around flaunting his job-related scars as some of his fellow firefighters did, he still regarded them as badges of professional honor. Except for the ones that pockmarked his left buttock, that is. Those particular scars he regarded as an acute embarrassment.

Phoebe had spotted his old wounds four days ago. The two of them had just finished showering after their morning run. He'd been reaching for a towel when he'd heard her gasp.

He'd understood the reason for the shocked sound as soon as he'd pivoted to face her. The direction of her gaze had been self-explanatory.

"It's not what it looks like," he'd said quickly.

Phoebe had lifted her eyes to his, her brows arching halfway to her hairline. "What it looks like is that you took a load of buckshot in the rear end."

The bluntly worded diagnosis had been right on target. This had startled Jackson for a second, then he'd remembered Phoebe's medical training. She'd once told him that her internship had included a stint in an emergency room.

"Well, actually, yeah," he'd admitted with a grimace, recalling some of the ribbing he'd taken from his colleagues after he'd sustained the wounds. "But don't go imagining I was running away from an outraged husband or anything like that. It happened about four years ago, during a two-alarm call at a condo in Buckhead."

"Are you saying somebody *shot* you while you were trying to do your job?"

"Oh, it wasn't deliberate. The owner of the condo was a gun collector. He had a box of shells sitting out on a table. When the shells got hot enough, they went off. I just happened to get caught in the line of fire."

"Good God."

"That's one of the scary things about residential alarms," he'd continued frankly. "You never know what you're going to run into. People keep all kinds of stuff around their houses. Gasoline. Kerosene. Paint thinner. Heck, I've seen ordinary aerosol spray cans go off like grenades a couple of times. Plus, most homes are full of plastic. That usually means toxic fumes and dirty smoke."

Phoebe had stared at him, obviously appalled by what she'd just heard. "Were you . . . were you badly hurt when you were shot?"

He'd shrugged. "Well, I sure didn't feel like sitting down for a few weeks after it happened. My pride took the worst of it, though. I mean, if you get shot in the backside, you tend to become the butt of a lot of jokes."

The sound of Phoebe's voice prodded Jackson back into the present.

"Well?" she queried. "Do exploding semibaked potatoes sound anything like exploding shotgun shells?"

Jackson gazed at her for a few seconds, enjoying the sassy expression on her upturned face. "I tell you what, darlin'," he finally said. "If you don't mention the buckshot in my behind again, I'll keep quiet about last night's dinner."

Phoebe tilted her head to one side and appeared to consider this proposal. Then she smiled. "Deal."

"Deal," Jackson echoed. Leaning forward, he brushed her mouth with his own.

The kiss was meant to be quick and casual. But as their lips caught and clung, it deepened into a passionate caress. Jackson encircled Phoebe with his arms and drew her against him. She went up on tiptoes, opening her mouth to the delving stroke of his tongue.

Yes, he thought, cupping the curve of her bottom with one hand and the back of her head with the other. Oh, yes.

Eventually the kiss came to an end and they eased apart. They stood, staring at each other.

"What about the chicken?" Phoebe finally asked. Her voice was husky, her cheeks flushed. The thrust of her nipples was obvious beneath the stretchy fabric of her tank top.

"The . . . chicken?" Jackson repeated blankly.

"The chicken we're supposed to be frying."

"Oh. That. What . . . what about it?"

"Shall I get it out of the refrigerator?"

"Sure." He nodded. "Good idea."

The chicken had been soaking in a bowl of Tabasco-spiked milk for about an hour. Phoebe retrieved the bowl from the refrigerator and brought it back to the counter where they were working.

"And now?" she prompted as she set the container down.

"Now you dredge each piece of chicken in the flour."

"That, I think I can manage." Phoebe fished a plump breast out of the bowl and dragged it through the coating mixture.

"You need to massage it, darlin'."

"Massage . . . the chicken?"

"Just a bit."

"I'm not sure—"

"Here." Jackson stepped behind Phoebe, positioning her between himself and the edge of the counter. He reached around her. "Let me help you."

They worked together for several minutes. What little space there had been between their bodies quickly disappeared. Whether this was due to Phoebe snuggling back against him or to him shifting forward against her, Jackson was never able to say. All he knew was that he was feeling a little dizzy by the time they finished coating the last piece of poultry. Given that a large percentage of his blood seemed to have been rerouted from his brain to the hardening rod of male flesh between his thighs, he supposed such light-headedness was inevitable.

After a moment or two, Phoebe turned around. Well, actually, *squirmed* around was a more accurate description. "Tell me, Lieutenant Miller," she said throatily, tilt-

ng her chin and gazing up at him. "Is that a drumstick in
our pocket...or are you happy to see me?"

Jackson's pulse started doing cartwheels. He grinned.
"What do you think, darlin'?"

"Well..." The expression in Phoebe's gold-sparked green
eyes was enticing. The flutter of her fingertips against the
front of his jeans was incendiary.

Jackson's grin gave way to an involuntary growl of response. For an instant he was genuinely afraid he might lose
control of his body in a way he hadn't done since the first
time he'd gotten a full-palmed feel of a naked female breast.
He captured Phoebe's hand in a convulsive clasp. Her hand
stilled for a mind-blowing moment, then slowly began to
curve and cup....

Oh, God.

Oh, God.

He kissed her. Once. Twice. Three times. The mating of
their mouths was hot and hungry. Jackson nipped at the
curve of Phoebe's lower lip. She raked his tongue with the
delicately serrated edge of her front teeth.

"Oh, Jackson..."

"Oh, Phoebe..."

They kissed again. Jackson tugged at Phoebe's tank top,
freeing it from the waistband of her snug-fitting shorts. He
pushed the garment upward, caressing her newly bared
flesh. She quivered in answer to his touch, then began un-
buttoning his shirt.

They'd shed most of their clothes by the time Phoebe returned to the question she'd asked earlier.

"What...about...the chicken?"

The answer Jackson whispered in her ear was as explicit
as it was succinct.

Phoebe made a sound that was midway between a laugh
and a gasp. "Oh, no," she protested, shaking her head. Her
flame-colored hair, which had been freed from the confine-

ment of its ponytail a few seconds earlier, swayed against her
face and over her shoulders. "You're supposed to do that to
me."

Barely a minute later, Jackson did.

Ten

Phoebe paused in the act of bringing a bite of eggplant parmigiana to her mouth and stared at the strikingly attractive black woman sitting across the table. She slowly lowered her fork to her plate. "Fridge has asked you to marry him?"

"Uh-huh." Keezia Carew extracted a chunk of bread from the wicker basket sitting between them. She broke it into several pieces and began using the smallest one to mop up the marinara sauce remaining on her plate. "Three times."

"And you've turned him down?"

Keezia nodded, popping the sauce-soaked morsel of bread into her mouth. She chewed, swallowed, then asked, "Aren't you going to tell me I'm out of my mind?"

The question surprised Phoebe. So did the defensive tone in which it was asked. "Why should I tell you that, Keezia?"

"Why shouldn't you?" The black woman made a face. "Everybody else I know has."

"Well, don't go adding me to the list of those questioning your sanity just yet."

Keezia studied Phoebe for a moment or two. Then her lips parted in a crooked smile. *"That*'s a relief to hear. Having ordinary folks call me crazy is one thing. Having it come from a bona fide psychiatrist..."

There was another pause. Phoebe finished up the last few mouthfuls of her entrée.

Keezia and Fridge, she mused. Quite a couple.

She'd sensed there was something between the two almost from the first moment she'd seen them together at the Show and Muster. And now that she'd had nearly a month to get to know the pair—

"You're starting to wonder," Keezia accused dryly.

Phoebe blinked. "Wonder?"

"About whether my saying 'no' to Fridge might mean I'm a taco shy of a combination plate."

"No," Phoebe denied with a laugh. "I'm not."

Keezia cocked her close-cropped head. "But you *are* trying to figure out why I'd refuse his proposal."

Phoebe lifted her wineglass and took a drink. "It's obvious Fridge means a great deal to you," she responded, opting to sidle up to the issue rather than confront it head-on.

Keezia sat up very straight. Her gem-toned eyes glinted with emotion. "Ralph Randall is the best man I've ever known."

"But you don't want to marry him." Phoebe kept her voice gentle and nonjudgmental.

There was a tense silence. The light faded from Keezia's eyes. "No," she finally agreed. "I don't."

A question trembled on the tip of Phoebe's tongue. She forced herself to swallow it. Although she and Keezia had become good friends in a surprisingly short time, she was wary of venturing into personal territory, even though it seemed she was being invited to do so.

Keezia sighed and lowered her gaze. She began fingering the stem of her wineglass. "If I married anybody, it'd be Fridge," she said after nearly a minute. "It's just that..."

A second sigh. More fiddling with the wineglass. Finally she looked up at Phoebe. "You know I'm divorced, right?"

"You mentioned something about it last weekend," Phoebe, Jackson, Keezia and Fridge had gone out together the previous Sunday night. During the course of the very enjoyable evening, Keezia had made a passing reference to having an ex-husband who lived somewhere up north.

Keezia sighed for a third time. "The thing is, my marriage got pretty ugly before I finally found the guts to get out. Tyrell—that was my husband's name, Tyrell Babcock—knocked me around. He knocked me around...a lot."

"Oh, Keezia." Phoebe leaned forward.

"I bought into everything Tyrell laid on me for nearly three years," the woman went on. "Including the idea that his beating me was my fault. Then one morning I looked into the bathroom mirror and saw a woman I didn't recognize. She had a black eye and a split lip and she was wearing the kind of expression you usually see in zombie movies. After a few seconds I realized that this woman—this *stranger*—was me. And, well, I'm not certain how to explain what happened next. But all of a sudden, this little voice inside me started saying, 'This isn't right, girl. You haven't done anything to deserve this. Even if you're as worthless as Tyrell keeps telling you—which you know in your soul you aren't—you *do not* deserve to be treated this way.'"

"And you walked out?"

Keezia nodded. "I packed my things and went home to my mother. Tyrell came after me and tried to cause trouble, but I called the police on him and pressed charges. Then I got a lawyer and filed for divorce. I joined one of those support groups for battered women, too. Six months later, Tyrell was serving time for assault and I was freer than I'd been in a long, long time."

"That's remarkable," Phoebe said sincerely, understanding how difficult it must have been for Keezia to affect the transformation just described. She'd dealt with abuse victims throughout her professional career. She knew the kind of courage and strength it took to break the cycle of emotional or physical violence.

Keezia shrugged, apparently uncomfortable with the praise. "What's remarkable is that in the four years since I showed up on her doorstep, my mother's never said, 'I told you so, Keezia Lorraine.' Lord knows, she's had every right to. She warned me Tyrell Babcock was bad news from the get-go. But she's never reminded me of that. Not once." Keezia pulled a face. "Of course, she *is* leading the chorus of folks who're telling me I'm nuts for not marrying Fridge."

"It takes a long time to recover from the kind of experience you went through, Keezia," Phoebe said seriously. "And you're the only one who can gauge how that recovery process is going. If you don't think you're ready to make a commitment—"

"There are times when I want to marry him," Keezia interrupted, the words coming out in a rush. "But then I get scared. Really, truly scared. I know with my head and my heart that Fridge is nothing—*nothing!*—like Tyrell. Still, I can't help thinking that if I was a fool for love once, I might be a fool for love again."

Phoebe frowned. "Are you afraid Fridge might abuse you?"

"No!" The sincerity of the denial was palpable. "Oh, Lord, no. He's never even raised his *voice* to me. It's just that . . . that . . . oh, I don't know how to explain it, Phoebe! Maybe I could get over whatever it is that's messing me up if he wasn't so damned big. Because every once in a while, I flash on what it would be like if a man of his size laid into me the way Tyrell did."

"Have you talked about this with Fridge?"

Keezia nodded. "And he's been so sweet. But I know it hurts him. Knowing I get frightened of him sometimes, I mean. And that makes *me* hurt."

Their waiter—a young man who'd introduced himself earlier as Mario—chose that particular moment to materialize by their table.

"May I get you ladies some dessert?" he inquired as he began clearing their plates.

It took Phoebe a moment to shift conversational gears from the intensely emotional to the utterly mundane. "Ah, no, thank you," she replied.

"I'm fine, too," Keezia declared.

"Cappuccino?" Mario offered. "Espresso?"

Phoebe checked her watch. She and Keezia were planning on going to the eight-thirty showing of a movie. It was now a few minutes past eight.

"None for me," her dining companion refused. "Phoebe?"

"None for me, either. If we could get our check, please?"

Mario nodded. "Sure. I'll be back with that in just a minute."

"So, what about you?" Keezia asked as the waiter hustled away.

"Me?" Phoebe patted her mouth with her napkin.

"You and Jackson. I'm done pouring out my heart for the evening. It's your turn to give."

Phoebe hesitated, her mind suddenly replaying a fragment of conversation from her first date with Jackson.

"Is something wrong?" she'd asked.

"No," he'd replied. *"I was just thinking what a good listener you are."*

"Thank you," she'd answered, a bit wary of the compliment.

"I suppose you have to be, given what you do for a living," he'd gone on.

"Well..."

"You don't seem very comfortable when it comes to reciprocity, though."

"I'm not certain what to say, Keezia," she answered after few moments.

"I'm not asking for X-rated details." The woman's tone was teasing. "Even though it's obvious to anyone with any sense that you and Jackson have been doing the nasty."

Phoebe smiled at the slang, a *frisson* of remembered ecstasy skittering up her spine. "Actually, what Jackson and I have been doing has been very nice," she said demurely.

Keezia gave a throaty laugh. "Girl, if the look on your lily-white face is anything to go by, it's been a lot better than *that!*"

"Mmm..."

"Are you two getting serious?"

The directness of the question caught Phoebe off guard. She averted her gaze, unable—or unwilling—to answer it right away.

Were she and Jackson getting serious?

She was in love with the man, for heaven's sake! It was difficult to imagine anything more "serious" than that. She loved Jackson Stuart Miller and she truly believed she was learning to cope with the fears that emotion stirred within her. Whether she would ever reach the point where she could confess to and conquer those fears, she couldn't say.

Nor could she say whether her love was returned. That Jackson liked her—that he enjoyed her company in and out of bed—was clear. But he'd given no sign he wanted to deepen or expand their relationship. And to be quite honest, she wasn't sure how she would have responded if he had.

"Phoebe?" Keezia prompted.

Phoebe looked across the table. "I...I don't know."

"You don't know about you? Or you don't know about him?"

"I don't know about either of us."

Keezia frowned. "You care about Jackson, don't you?"

Phoebe's throat seemed to close up. She nodded.

"And he cares about you."

"I suppose."

"You *suppose?*"

"He's never said anything, Keezia."

The other woman arched her brows. "It's not what a man says, Phoebe. It's what he does."

"Fridge has told you how he feels, hasn't he?"

"That's different," came the ricochet-quick response. "But don't go trying to change the subject on me. We're talking about *you*."

There was an uncomfortable pause.

"Jackson tells me I do that a lot," Phoebe said quietly.

"What?"

"Try to shift conversations off me and onto somebody else."

"Do you?"

Phoebe sighed. "Yes," she conceded honestly. "I never realized it until Jackson called me on it. But yes, I do."

"It's usually the other way around. Most people try to shift the subject off others and onto themselves."

"I guess I'm not 'most people.'"

"I don't think Jackson would be interested in you if you were."

The confidence in this assertion sparked an odd tremor in Phoebe. "Has he said something to you, Keezia?" she asked, wishing she didn't feel such a need for reassurance.

Keezia seemed to consider the question very carefully. Then she shook her head. "Not the way you mean, no. But I've got eyes, Phoebe. I've seen the two of you together."

"Has he said something to Fridge?"

"About you?"

"Yes."

"Probably."

"You don't *know?*"

"No. And I wouldn't try to find out, either. Fridge and Jackson have been working side by side for nearly ten years. They couldn't get any tighter if you glued them together. What they talk about when I'm not around..." The woman spread her hands, palms up.

"Fridge knew who I was the first time we met," Phoebe recalled. "So did you, for that matter."

Keezia's mouth quirked. "If you're wondering whether you've been a topic of discussion at the station, the answer is yes. The scuttlebutt started flying back in June, after the fire that burned up the building you were living in. Word got around that Jackson went out of channels to find out who you were. And then, barely a week later, you moved in with him."

"I didn't 'move in' with him. I rented an apartment from him."

"Close enough."

Phoebe grimaced. "I can just imagine the kind of talk my visiting the firehouse must have caused."

"Well, most of the guys had already gotten a chance to check you out at the Show and Muster." The comment was matter-of-fact. "Still, you *did* stir up a certain amount of—"

"Here you are, ladies," Mario the waiter interrupted, placing their bill on the table. "Sorry about the delay."

"Can I ask you something personal, Phoebe?" Keezia inquired as they headed for the restaurant's exit a few minutes later.

"More personal than whether Jackson and I are doing the nasty?"

"I never asked that. I just assumed you were."

Phoebe smiled fleetingly, recalling what else Keezia had assumed. "I stand corrected. Ask away."

"What would you do if Jackson asked you to marry him?"

"Do you think they're talkin' about us tonight?"

"Who? Phoebe and Keezia?"

"Yeah."

"Probably. What do you think?"

"There isn't a doubt in my mind."

The time was shortly before 10:00 p.m. on what had been an exceptionally quiet Sunday. Jackson and Fridge were sitting in front of their firehouse in lawn chairs, shooting the bull and enjoying the balmy night air. Many of the other members of the A-shift crew were asleep in their bunks.

Jackson had been contemplating hitting the sack, too. The problem was, he wasn't tired. There'd only been one call since he'd come on duty and that had been a false alarm.

"How's it going with you and Keezia?" he asked after a bit, forking his fingers back through his hair.

Fridge sighed gustily. "Same old, same old. She's still dealin' with what that bastard she was married to did to her. God, I hate that son of a bitch! I know it isn't Christian, but I really do."

Jackson nodded his understanding. He was familiar with the story of Keezia's unfortunate marriage. She'd confided it to Fridge and Fridge had related it to him.

"Tyrell Babcock will get his one of these days," he said flatly. "As for Keezia, she's got a lot to get behind her, man. Give her time."

"Oh, I intend to, Jackson. I just wish she'd let me help her more, you know?"

"Hey. She's an independent woman."

Fridge gave a rumbling laugh. The sound held equal parts of frustration and affection. "You've got that right."

There was a brief silence. Fridge shifted his position again, stretching his legs out in front of him. "Speakin' of independent women," he resumed. "How're things with you and Phoebe?"

Jackson felt a peculiar little twist in the pit of his stomach when he heard the word *things*. "Good question," he returned after a moment or two.

"Got any good answers?"

"Not yet."

"Uh-huh. You still tryin' to understand her?"

Jackson gestured. "I'm doing my best."

Fridge shifted his position again. "I've said it before and I'll say it again. If the good Lord had meant for men to understand women, He would have put the explanation in writing."

"You seem to understand Keezia pretty well."

"Oh, I understand her just fine when she's on the job, actin' like a firefighter. But the rest of the time? Give me a break. I feel like I'm stumblin' around in a mine field at midnight."

Jackson sighed and tilted his head back. "I hear you."

A pause.

"You're goin' to have to make some kind of decision pretty soon, Jackson," Fridge eventually commented. There was an unusual edge in his deep voice. "Unless you're plannin' to keep carryin' on with Phoebe after Lauralee comes home from Baltimore?"

Jackson went rigid. He didn't think for an instant that his friend's choice of words had been accidental. The inquiry had been honed like an ax. And the man who'd uttered it was an expert at wielding sharpened blades.

"What kind of question is that, Fridge?" he demanded. "God Almighty! Carrying on? I have a relationship with Phoebe the same way you have a relationship with Keezia!"

"I don't think so" came the quick, cutting retort. "'Cuz in *my* relationship, I've asked the lady to marry me."

Jackson opened his mouth to respond but shut it when he realized there was no way of defending himself against the truth. Whatever their problems, Ralph Randall was committed to Keezia Carew for keeps. Whereas his commitment to Phoebe was... was—

What? Had he even made one? Did he really *want* to make one?

"I don't... I don't know if I'm ready for this, Jackson," she'd told him hours after she'd provided the physical and emotional solace he'd so desperately needed.

"I don't know if I'm ready for this, either," he'd answered. *"Whatever 'this' is. But I'd like to find out..."*

Three weeks had gone by since that exchange. Twenty-one days and nights. Yet despite the passage of time, Jackson still couldn't explain what "this" was. Not to himself. And certainly not to anybody else.

That his feelings for Phoebe were as powerful as any he'd ever experienced, he wasn't going to deny. But they were so damned *confusing!* The lady herself remained very much a puzzle to him. Open one moment, aloof the next. Generous in ways he'd never expected, yet always seeming to be holding something back.

And the questions she kept asking! Anne had never picked at him. Or probed at him. Anne had just...accepted. Phoebe, on the other hand—

"Hey, Jackson?"

Jackson turned his head. "Yeah?"

"I didn't mean to rile you, brother."

"Sure you did," Jackson retorted, easing back into the reassuring rhythm of a friendship that was nearly a decade old.

Fridge chuckled, his teeth flashing against his dark skin. "Well, maybe just a little. But it was for your own good."

"Uh-huh. And I'm sure it hurt you much more than it hurt me."

Another chuckle. "Oh, definitely."

A few moments slipped by. Jackson exhaled on a long, slow sigh. "You're right, you know," he finally admitted.

"About what?"

"I *do* have to make a decision about Phoebe."

An instant later, the station's alarm began to shrill.

"Do you know what I truly loved about that movie?" Keezia inquired, her eyes sparkling.

"The fact that the lead actor took off all his clothes—twice?" Phoebe guessed through a mouthful of key lime pie.

The black woman laughed and forked up a bite of cherry cheesecake. "Besides that."

Phoebe took a moment to clear her throat, then said, "Frankly, I thought the whole thing was great. It was terrific to see a film about a woman who succeeds without behaving like a bitch or a bimbo."

"Exactly!" An emphatic nod. "And she didn't have to blow anybody away in the process, either. Not that I think she wouldn't have been able to. I mean, that lady was one tough cop."

"*Very* tough."

Phoebe and Keezia were seated at a small table in a café in the Buckhead section of Atlanta. The place was remarkably busy for 11:00 p.m. on a Sunday. One of the main attractions seemed to be a big-screen color television bracketed to the wall behind the bar. Phoebe had noted the crowd clustered in front of it when she and Keezia had come in. Although she was now positioned with her back to them, she

could hear the gathered patrons exclaiming over whateve
it was they were watching.

"I thought about joining the police department," Keezi;
volunteered after a moment.

"Really?"

"Uh-huh. I took the entrance exam for it the same montl
I took the one for the fire department. Passed both of 'em
too."

"What made you choose firefighting?"

"Lots of different things. Public image, for one."

"Public image?"

Keezia speared another bite of cheesecake. "Folks genu
inely like firefighters. They see one coming, they feel good
Firefighters do things like rescuing people and saving prop
erty. But folks see a cop and they figure somebody's goin;
to get in trouble. Even if that somebody isn't them, it trig
gers negative associations. I mean, have you ever heard o
firefighter brutality? Or of some innocent bystander get
ting hosed down by accident?"

"I get your point."

"I'll also admit I liked the idea of helping break dowr
some stereotypes about what women supposedly can an
can't do."

Phoebe nodded. Given what she'd been through, it mad
sense that Keezia would seek a dramatic way to assert her
self—and to restore her self-esteem. "How many wome
firefighters are there in Atlanta?"

"Less than two dozen, last time I checked. There wer
only fourteen when I joined."

"That's not very many."

"Especially when you consider there's about nine hun
dred active firefighters in the department."

Phoebe digested this information as she ate another bit
of pie. Then she asked, "Where do you see your career go
ing?"

"I'm still working on that," Keezia returned. "I know
want to do more than haul hose between now and retire

ment. I'm ambitious. I want to move up in rank, take on more responsibility."

"Is it difficult to get promoted?" Phoebe was genuinely curious. "Jackson's been in the department for fourteen years and he's only a lieutenant."

Keezia laughed. "Phoebe, there are lieutenants and there are *lieutenants*. Jackson Miller could make captain like—" she snapped her fingers "—if he decided to. I know for a fact that the top brass keeps talking to him about taking a slot at the training academy." She paused, her expression growing thoughtful. "He could do a lot of good there, teaching what he knows. Jackson has a *gift* for firefighting. Maybe it's in his genes. Or maybe he takes the job more personally than a lot of us because of what happened to his father. But he's about the best in the department and everybody knows it."

"He loves his work," Phoebe said quietly.

Keezia tilted her head to one side, her topaz-colored eyes narrowing. "Is that a problem for you?"

Phoebe sustained her friend's scrutiny for several seconds, then lowered her gaze. "What he does scares me," she admitted tautly. "I don't want to...I mean, the possibility that something might happen—"

"Oh, dear God."

The horror in Keezia's voice brought Phoebe's head up with a jerk. The woman was staring in the direction of the bar. The expression on her face made Phoebe's stomach clench. She turned around.

Her breath wedged at the top of her throat as she focused on the television behind the bar. A local news reporter was on the screen. There was a huge fire raging behind him.

"Turn it up!" Keezia called.

Heads swung in their direction.

"Dammit! Turn the sound up!"

"...out of control," the television suddenly blared. "Three firefighters are confirmed dead. At least two others have been seriously injured—"

Phoebe pivoted back toward Keezia, her heart pounding, her stomach churning. "Keezia—?"

"I know the building" came the stark reply. "It's a construction company warehouse and it's in our zone. Fridge and Jackson are at that fire."

Eleven

'**A**shes to ashes..."

Phoebe had seen grown men cry before. But the masculine tears she'd witnessed in the course of various therapy sessions had left her largely unaffected. The ones she saw being shed at the funeral of twenty-two-year-old Probationary Fire Officer Dwight Daniels had a very different impact on her. The sight of scores of veteran members of the Atlanta Fire Department weeping for a fallen comrade moved her deeply.

Dwight Daniels was one of the three firefighters who'd died in Sunday night's warehouse blaze. Like the other two victims, he'd been killed by the explosion of several drums of industrial solvent.

A newspaper account Phoebe had read the day after the tragedy had quoted a witness as saying the explosion had sounded like a "bomb blast." The witness had also professed astonishment that anyone who'd been inside the warehouse had made it out alive.

Phoebe had met "Probie" Daniels the Friday night she'
visited Jackson's station. She'd sat next to him during di
ner. Although the young firefighter had seemed painfull
shy at first, he'd gradually relaxed and had begun respon
ing to her conversational gambits with something more a
ticulate than stammered, single syllable answers. By the er
of the meal, she'd learned that he'd been married for les
than a year and was due to become a father around th
middle of November. She'd also deduced that he abso
lutely idolized Lieutenant Jackson Stuart Miller.

"Dust to dust..."

Jackson was standing to Phoebe's right. Biting her lowe
lip to control a sudden quiver, she slanted a look at him
Like his fellow firefighters, he was wearing an impeccabl
pressed dress uniform. The well-polished badge pinned
his chest was banded with a narrow strip of black ribbon.

Although the expression on his tanned, strong-boned fac
was full of grief, Jackson's compelling blue eyes were dr
His gaze was fixed on the silver-haired minister who wa
conducting the solemn graveside service.

"Let us pray," the cleric intoned.

Phoebe drew a shaky breath. Her head throbbed sicker
ingly as she tried to fend off a single, nightmarish truth.

It could have been Jackson.

It could have been Jackson!

Phoebe clenched her hands.

It could have been Jackson who'd been killed in Sunda
night's fire. It could have been him, not young Dwigh
Daniels, who so many people had gathered to mourn.

Or it could have been him, not Fridge Randall, who'
ended up in the Intensive Care Unit of a hospital. The blac
firefighter had suffered third-degree burns, internal in
juries and several broken bones when a ceiling beam ha
come crashing down on him. Jackson had freed him fron
the debris and carried him to safety.

Phoebe had heard the basic story of Fridge's narrow es
cape at the scene of the fire. She and Keezia had driven ther
after seeing the television report at the café. Keezia ha

quickly located someone she knew and pleaded to be told what was going on.

"Then Fridge is alive?" she'd demanded when the firefighter she'd buttonholed had finished speaking. "You're sure?"

The firefighter had given a rasping cough and wiped his mucus-streaming nostrils with the back of one hand. "He was breathin' when they put him in the ambulance, Keezia," he'd said hoarsely. "That's all I know."

"And Jackson?" Phoebe had asked, her throat tight.

The firefighter had coughed again, then jerked a bandaged thumb in the direction of the burning warehouse. "Workin'."

Phoebe and Keezia had raced from the fire site to the hospital to which Fridge and a second firefighter, a lieutenant named Lewis Finster, had been transported. Once at the medical facility, Phoebe hadn't hesitated to use her status as a doctor to obtain information about the condition of the two injured men. The news—what little of it there had been—had not been good. Fridge had been rushed into an operating room within minutes of his arrival. The other firefighter, who'd sustained some type of head trauma, had been taken into surgery, too.

Phoebe had spent the rest of the night keeping an anxious vigil with Keezia. They'd been joined in their long wait by Fridge's mother, Helen, plus Lewis Finster's wife and two teenage sons. More than a dozen off-duty members of the Atlanta Fire Department had also shown up to offer aid and comfort.

Phoebe had been touched by the way the firefighters had rallied to support their own. Yet she'd detected a certain fatalism in the outpouring of compassion. Looking around the waiting room, she'd sensed that each man present had been aware there might come a time when *he* would be the one fighting for his life on an operating table.

The hours had dragged by. Phoebe had prayed as she'd never prayed before.

Lewis Finster had come out of surgery first. The prognosis had been encouraging. His wife had broken down

when she'd received the news. Her sons, who'd obviously
expected her to be as relieved as they were, had stood by in
shocked bewilderment as she'd collapsed into a chair and
begun weeping with near-hysterical intensity. After a brief
hesitation, Phoebe had stepped in and taken control of the
situation. Calming the woman hadn't been easy, but she'd
done it.

Fridge's surgery had ended nearly two hours later. While
the surgeon who'd handled the case had been grimly honest when he'd explained the extent of his patient's injuries,
he'd also stressed Fridge's physical resilience and will to live.

"The next twenty-four hours will be crucial," the doctor—with whom Phoebe had a passing professional ac-
quaintance—had concluded. "But he's a real fighter. I could
tell that on the table. And when a patient won't give up,
well, let's just say the human spirit can be as important as
medical science in this kind of case."

"My boy's a survivor," Fridge's mother had declared
quietly.

"Fridge is strong," Keezia had agreed in a husky voice,
her exotic golden eyes glistening with tears. "And we're going to be with him every step of the way."

Helen Randall had put a comforting arm around the
younger woman. "When can we see him?"

The surgeon had glanced at Phoebe, his brows slightly
elevated. She'd known he'd been wondering about the ad-
visability of allowing Helen and Keezia to look in on Fridge
while he was still in the recovery room. She'd responded to
his unspoken question with a tiny nod, confident that the
two most important women in Ralph Randall's life could
cope with the unpleasant reality of his postoperative situation.

"You can see him right now," the doctor had replied,
transferring his gaze back to the two women. "But only for
a few moments. After that, I'd strongly suggest that both of
you take a break and get some rest."

"I'll stay here," Phoebe had said. "I need to phone the
hospital and let my department chief know I'm going to be
late for work."

Jackson had arrived roughly five minutes later. Phoebe had just finished her call when she'd heard him say her name. She'd whirled, her pulse scrambling, tears springing to her eyes. Within the space of a single heartbeat, she'd been in his arms.

"Jackson." She'd hugged him fiercely, desperate to reassure herself that he was truly there and truly all right. She'd buried her face against his broad chest. He'd stunk of smoke and sweat. "Oh, Jackson."

He'd embraced her with tender force, stroking her hair with hands that weren't quite steady. Finally he'd eased back a bit.

"Fridge?" he'd asked, gazing down at her with red-rimmed, bloodshot eyes.

"He's out of surgery," she'd answered, wishing she could do something to smooth the deep lines that furrowed his brow and bracketed his mouth. "His condition's critical but stable."

Jackson's angular jaw had fretted. "He's tough," he'd said after a few moments, his voice as scratchy as barbed wire. "He'll make it."

Phoebe had lifted her right hand and caressed her lover's beard-stubbled cheek. "I hear you saved his life."

Jackson had shaken his head, clearly disavowing any special claim to courage. "I just did my job. Fridge would have done the same—"

An anguished cry jerked Phoebe out of the past and back into the present. The source of the sorrow-filled sound was Dwight Daniels's widow. She'd been standing to the left of the minister along with a somberly clad couple Jackson had earlier identified as Dwight's parents.

"D-Dwight," the young woman said in a tremulous voice, taking a step toward her husband's casket. She swayed, pressing her palms protectively against her swollen belly. "Oh, *Dwight.*"

Everyone seemed to freeze. Even the minister stopped speaking. Then Dwight's father moved forward and took his daughter-in-law gently by the arm. "It will be all right, Katie," he said soothingly. "It's all right, honey."

The young woman turned to him. "How can...how c-can you say that?" Her voice quavered. "Dwight's gone, Daddy Daniels. He's *gone*. I loved him so m-much. I loved him...and now I've lost him forever. He promised m-me, you know. What with the b-baby comin' and all, he promised me he would be...c-c-careful. Why...why d-didn't...why didn't h-he...?"

Phoebe lowered her gaze as Katie Daniels collapsed, sobbing, against her father-in-law. Her chest felt as though it had been banded with unyielding strips of steel.

I can't, she thought, blinking against a sudden rush of tears. *I just can't do it.*

Yes, Jackson had survived Sunday night's disaster unscathed. But there were going to be other fires. And when there were, she knew the man she loved would be one of the brave souls rushing forward to battle the flames while everybody else was fleeing from them. She knew he would be risking his life, over and over....

To love.

To lose.

She couldn't go through it, not again. She couldn't even endure the possibility of going through it.

Phoebe lifted her head slowly, then looked to her right. Her breath wedged at the top of her throat as her gaze locked with Jackson's. The expression in his sky-colored eyes was one she'd never seen before. She had the unnerving impression he was peering directly into her soul.

She felt him take her right hand with his left one. She trembled at his touch. The tears she'd tried so hard to hold back began to fall.

To love.

To lose.

It could have been Jackson.

In the moment before Phoebe's fingers intertwined with those of the man to whom she'd given her heart, she made up her mind what she had to do.

He loved her.

It was one hell of a realization to come to in the middle of

a funeral, Jackson acknowledged as he gazed deep into
Phoebe's wide green eyes. But there it was.

Then again, perhaps the timing of the revelation wasn't
quite as perverse as it seemed. What was it Phoebe had told
him in the tumultuous aftermath of their becoming lovers?
Something about affirming life and human impulses—

Oh, yes. Now he remembered.

*"What happened between us—our making love to-
gether—it was a natural thing,"* she'd said. *"Don't you see,
Jackson? The desire to affirm life in the face of death is a
very potent human impulse. It's a way of coping. This
morning, after the fire, you* needed *someone—"*

"No," he'd disputed, damming the flow of her words
with his fingers. *"I needed* you, *Phoebe. I wanted* you.
Not...someone. You."

He'd loved her then, but he hadn't been ready to accept
the true nature of his feelings. Now, at long last, he was.

For reasons he couldn't begin to explain, Jackson suddenly flashed back on the memory of his father's funeral.
The image of his mother's face filled his mind. She hadn't
cried, he recalled with a profound sense of surprise. She
hadn't cried once. And because she hadn't wept, neither had
he.

The past dissolved into the present. Jackson saw tears on
Phoebe's pale cheeks. His own eyes grew moist. I love you,
darlin', he thought.

Reaching out, he clasped Phoebe's right hand with his
left. He felt her quiver at the contact. A split second later,
her fingers began to lace with his. In that moment, Jackson
made up his mind what he was going to do.

Deciding exactly when and how he was going to do it took
a bit longer.

"Please. Don't."

Jackson lowered his arms and stepped back, temporarily
abandoning his effort to embrace Phoebe. Something wasn't
right. He'd spent more than twenty-four hours psyching

himself up for this moment. A physical rebuff had not been included in any of the scenarios he'd envisioned.

Heaven knew, Phoebe had been more than eager for his touch the previous night! Although she'd been understandably pensive following Dwight Daniels's funeral, her mood had turned passionate after they'd returned home. She'd enticed. Incited. Been totally without inhibition. Even now, the memory of what they'd done together made him feel a little weak in the knees.

Jackson took a deep breath. Maybe he should wait.

No, he told himself. He wasn't going to put it off. He loved Phoebe and he was going to ask her to become his wife, just the way he'd planned.

He had the ring. A diamond solitaire, picked out and purchased that afternoon.

He had his daughter's endorsement, too. He'd phoned her right after Phoebe had left for work. He'd intended to ease into the subject of his matrimonial plans gradually. Lauralee had had other ideas.

"Daddy," she'd interrupted him, her voice holding equal parts of affection, amusement and exasperation, "are you tryin' to tell me you're goin' to ask Phoebe to marry you?"

A uniquely paternal kind of astonishment had deprived him of the ability to speak for several seconds. "Well, uh, yeah, sugar," he'd eventually replied. "I was sort of, uh, working my way up to it."

A sigh had come down the line. He'd known Lauralee was shaking her head. "I sure hope you're not goin' to beat around the bush like this with Phoebe."

Jackson had raked his fingers though his hair at that point, taken aback by his daughter's tone. He'd never heard his little girl sound so grown up. He'd wondered fleetingly what had happened to the good old days when she'd believed him to be the font of all worldly wisdom.

"You think I should use the direct approach, hmm?" he'd finally asked.

"Oh, definitely."

"I, ah, take it you approve—"

Lauralee hadn't allowed him to finish the question. "Of course!" she'd exclaimed. "You and Phoebe are *perfect* together, Daddy. I knew it right from the start. I mean, it was like...like...*destiny*."

Jackson took another slow, steadying breath, weighing the word his daughter had used while he studied Phoebe's face.

Destiny...

He thought back to the first time he'd seen her. To the visceral sense of recognition he'd experienced when their eyes had met. To the primitive kind of protectiveness he'd felt when she'd fainted into his arms.

Jackson still shied from the notion that fate—rather than his own free will—was determining the shape of his life. Yet he had to concede Lauralee's assessment of his relationship with Phoebe had a certain validity. There was something...inevitable...about their coming together.

"Rough day at the hospital, darlin'?" he asked.

"Yes." A shake of the head. "No." A grimace. "It doesn't matter."

Jackson quashed the impulse to inform Phoebe that it mattered very much. What was going on? he wondered uneasily. That the woman he loved tended to be closemouthed about her professional burdens was something he'd accepted—for the time being. But to have her slam the door on a simple inquiry about her day...

"Dinner won't be ready for a bit," he said after a few moments. He gestured toward the kitchen. "Would you like a drink? I've got some wine."

"No," Phoebe answered. Then, as though to temper the brusqueness of her refusal she added, "Thank you."

All right, he thought. No wine. She probably wasn't going to be receptive to the notion of going into the kitchen for a few pre-meal nibbles, either. Which left—what? She didn't seem to want to cuddle. She sure as hell didn't want to talk about what she'd done at work. Maybe he could—

"Jackson, there's something I need to say to you."

Phoebe's tone pulled him up short. Then the realization that she'd moved out of touching range slammed in. Off

balance, he responded to her statement with the unvar
nished truth. "There's something I need to say to you, too
Phoebe."

She stiffened. "What . . . what is it?"

He shook his head. "Ladies first."

Phoebe lowered her gaze. Jackson watched her draw a
deep breath, then square her shoulders. Finally she raised
her eyes to his and said with devastating simplicity, "We
can't go on the way we've been."

A crazy sense of relief spiraled through Jackson. The
woman he loved obviously had come to the same conclusion about their relationship that he had. And, independent woman that she was, she'd plainly decided to take the
initiative and act on that conclusion. Which was fine with
him—up to a point. While he viewed what he and Phoebe
had as a partnership of equals, he still had his masculine
pride. And that pride required an adherence to certain old-
fashioned traditions. Namely the traditions of *him* doing the
asking and *her,* the accepting.

"I know, darlin'," he said after a second or two.

"You do?"

Resisting the urge to reply "I do," Jackson reached into
the pocket of his trousers. He'd eschewed his usual off-duty
jeans this evening. It had seemed to him that a proposal of
marriage deserved something more formal than ordinary
denim.

"Lauralee told me I should use the direct approach," he
commented, taking out a velvet-covered jeweler's box and
extending it to Phoebe. "It's kind of humbling for a man to
find out his fifteen-year-old daughter is smarter than he is."

"Wh-what—?" Phoebe asked as she accepted the small,
snap-hinged cube. Her hands were as unsteady as her voice.

"Open it," Jackson urged.

She did. "No," she whispered, staring into the box. "Oh,
no."

"Hey." Jackson laughed uncomfortably. "Give me a
chance. I haven't even popped the question yet."

Phoebe lifted her gaze from the engagement ring to his
face. She opened her mouth to speak. A variety of emo-

tions—chief among them a sudden surge of foreboding—
prompted Jackson to rush to forestall her.

"I love you, Phoebe," he declared, taking a step forward. "I love you with all my heart and I want you to be my
wife. Will you...will you marry me?"

The blood drained from Phoebe's face. She swayed as
though she might faint. Jackson took a second step forward then froze when she made a gesture clearly intended to
ward him off. "Phoebe—" he began, appalled.

"I can't." She closed the jeweler's box with a *click*. There
was a terrible finality about the sound. "I—I didn't know,
Jackson. I mean, you never said—"

"What?" He cut in quickly. "That I love you? Oh, darlin'...darlin'. I never said it because I didn't understand
what I was feeling until yesterday. But now that I *do* understand, I'm ready to say it as many times as you want to hear
it. I'll say it over and over—" he swallowed hard, trying to
gauge her expression "—until you believe me."

"I believe you n-now," Phoebe replied, her voice catching on the last word. "But it doesn't—I can't marry you.
I...I can't even be with you anymore."

Jackson stared at the woman he loved. He felt numb. He
tried to speak. Once. Twice. Three times. Finally he managed to force out a single word. "Why?"

"Because I can't live with what you do."

Jackson shook his head. Her answer made no sense to
him. She couldn't live with what he *did?* What in the name
of heaven—

His breath jammed in his throat. His hands fisted of their
own volition. No, he thought. It wasn't possible, was it?

"Are you talking about my *job?*" he demanded. "About
my being a firefighter?"

Phoebe's answer, when it came, was a single syllable affirmative.

Something inside Jackson broke open, releasing a corro-
sive flood of anger and hurt. "Dammit, Phoebe!" He exploded. "How can you—you *knew!* You knew what I did
for a living from the moment we met!"

"Which is why I didn't want to get involved with you!" she flung back.

"What?"

Phoebe gestured. "I tried to steer clear of you, Jackson. You know I did! Only I couldn't. The attraction was too strong. So I succumbed to it. Then I realized I'd fallen in love with you, with a man who risks his life every time he goes to work. And it terrified me. But I tried to fight my fear. I tried to come to terms with your job, to understand why it matters so much to you. That's why I kept asking all those questions, why I wanted to visit the fire station. For a while, I thought it was going to be all right. I believed my love could overcome my fear. I believed it right up until Sunday night's fire. When I found out you were there— God!" Her eyes flashed. She clasped her hands to her breast. "It could have been *you,* Jackson. You could have been the one who ended up in a hospital bed, not Fridge or Lew Finster. You could have been the one who ended up in a grave—"

"Forget what could have been, Phoebe." Jackson closed the distance between them and caught her by the shoulders. He gave her a little shake. "I'm alive and well. I'm alive and well and *I love you!*"

"And I love you, Jackson!" she cried passionately. "But don't you understand? I loved my mother and she abandoned me when I was six years old. I loved my father and he died right in front of my eyes. I loved Alan Brinkley and he was killed less than a week before we were supposed to be married. He burned alive in a plane crash! Every time I care for someone, something terrible happens."

"Nothing is going to happen to me," he said fiercely, grappling with the implications of the loss-filled litany he'd just heard.

"You don't know that!" The coolly aloof lady psychiatrist was gone. In her place was a woman who seemed as vulnerable as an open wound.

"I promise you—"

"What?" Phoebe's voice turned shrill, shattering the word into anguished fragments of sound. "What do you promise me? The same thing Dwight Daniels promised his wife?"

He felt as though he'd been punched in the gut. "Darlin'..."

Phoebe wrenched free of his hands and took a step back. "That old saying about it being better to have loved and lost than to have never loved at all is wrong, Jackson. I've loved. I've lost. And I can't go through it again. I *can't.*"

"Can't?" Jackson countered harshly. "Or won't?"

"It's the same thing."

"No, it's not. Can't means you don't have any other other choice."

"I don't!"

"And yet you say you love me."

"I do. I *do* love you." Her throat worked convulsively. "I...I w-wish I d-didn't."

There was an awful, aching silence. Jackson drew a shuddery breath. He hadn't known a human being could experience such pain without screaming aloud in protest.

Finally Phoebe spoke again.

"I think I'd better go," she declared in a flat, uninflected voice. She held out the jeweler's box.

Jackson accepted the velvet-covered cube, his fingers closing around it with crushing force. "I won't try to stop you."

He didn't. But in the same instant Phoebe opened his front door to leave, he uttered her name. She stiffened, then slowly turned back to face him. There were tears trembling from the tips of her lashes.

"I've spent a lot of time trying to understand you," he said. "Too much, considering there's really only one thing I needed to know."

Phoebe blinked. A tear rolled down her right cheek, leaving a silvery trail on the milk-pale skin. "What's that?"

Jackson hurt. He wanted to hurt back.

"That you're a coward."

* * *

Lauralee Miller returned to Atlanta two days later. Phoebe was not at the airport to greet her.

When Jackson's teenage daughter came calling several hours after her arrival, Phoebe pretended she wasn't home.

Twelve

The classified ads in the *Atlanta Constitution* didn't appear to have changed much since the last time Phoebe had pored through them, searching for a place to live. Indeed, more than a few provoked an unsettling feeling of déjà vu within her.

A "cozy condo" near Emory University. She knew she'd read that one before.

A "luxuriously appointed town house" in Buckhead. She was pretty certain she'd seen that one, too. The rent specified seemed no less exorbitant now than it had ten and a half weeks ago.

The words "close to Inman Park" snagged her attention and tore at her heart. Phoebe inhaled sharply, trying to stave off a sudden urge to cry. It didn't matter that she knew the ad was for an apartment other than the one she currently occupied. But just the idea . . .

Jackson, she thought. Oh, God. *Jackson.*

Four days had passed since their disastrous confrontation in his living room. She hadn't seen him once during that period, except in her dreams. It was clear to her that Jackson was avoiding her as assiduously as she was avoiding him.

Had the love he'd professed for her turned to loathing? she wondered. She wouldn't be surprised if it had. The contempt she'd heard in his voice when he'd called her a coward had scalded her to the depths of her soul.

But she'd had no choice! She couldn't endure an existence predicated on the possibility of loss and that's what her life with Jackson would have been. She would have been afraid every moment of every day they were together. That fear would have eaten away at their relationship until there was nothing left. It would have eaten away at her, too.

She'd never expected an offer of marriage from Jackson. *Never.* Indeed, when Keezia Carew had asked her what her response to a proposal would be, her answer had been flippant yet heartfelt. "I'd faint," she'd said, then pointedly changed the subject.

She almost had passed out when she'd opened that velvet-covered jeweler's box. Lord, when she'd seen the unmistakable flash of diamond fire—

Phoebe shook her head, banishing the image of the engagement ring Jackson had offered from her mind. Blinking hard, she forced herself to focus on the newspaper once again. After a few moments, she extracted a pen from the clutter on top of her desk and drew lopsided circles around several ads. Then she reached for the phone. A split second later, it started to ring.

Phoebe started violently at the sound. She took a beat or two to steady herself, then picked up the receiver and put it to her ear. "Yes?"

"Dr. Donovan, this is the reception desk," a pleasant female voice informed her. "We've got a Lauralee Miller out here who'd like to see you."

Phoebe bit her lower lip. She'd known she was going to have to face Jackson's daughter sooner or later. The question was, was she ready to do it now?

The receptionist would cover for her, of course. That was one of the things receptionists did. She could instruct the woman to tell Lauralee—

Coward.

The word reverberated through Phoebe's brain.

"Dr. Donovan?" the receptionist pressed.

Phoebe cleared her throat. "Send her in, please."

There was a soft knock on her office door about a minute later.

"Come in," she called, getting to her feet.

Lauralee entered, chin up, shoulders squared, a very determined look on her pixie-pretty face. "Hi," she said solemnly, shutting the door behind her.

"Hi." Phoebe manufactured a smile, hoping it didn't look as synthetic as it felt. "I'm sorry I haven't had a chance to see you since you got back. It's just that I've been terribly busy here at the hospital and I've been working a lot of...a lot of..." A sudden change in Lauralee's expression made her lose the thread of her excuse. It was obvious the teenager hadn't believed one word she'd said. "Lauralee—"

"I'm not a stupid little k-kid, Phoebe," the girl declared, a small wobble entering her voice. "You don't have to make up lies for me. You didn't...you didn't u-used to."

A pang of shame lanced through Phoebe. She sank back into her seat. "I'm sorry," she apologized. She indicated the chair on the other side of her desk. "Please, sit down."

Lauralee did as she'd been bidden, keeping her spine straight and folding her hands demurely in her lap.

Phoebe drew a steadying breath. "So, what can I do for you?"

"You can tell me the truth."

"About—?"

"About what happened between you and Daddy."

Phoebe controlled an urge to look away. "What does your father say?"

The teenager grimaced and slumped down in her seat. "Nothin'."

"Nothing?" Phoebe's heart skipped a beat.

"Well, I know he asked you to marry him and you turned him down," Lauralee qualified. "See, Daddy called me in Baltimore last Friday to find out what I thought about his proposin' to you. And what I thought was that it would be wonderful. Only then, when I got home on Sunday, he said everythin' was off. That you weren't goin' to marry him. That you weren't even goin' to see him anymore. Naturally I wanted to know why. But he wouldn't say. I kept after him until he got angry and told me to mind my own business. The thing is, it *is* my business. I mean, you and Daddy breakin' up matters to me!''

"I understand that, Lauralee. But this isn't—"

"I'm not askin' for the really personal details, Phoebe.''

"I'm not sure—''

Jackson's daughter leaned forward abruptly, her blue eyes pleading. *"Please.''*

Phoebe exhaled on a sigh, surrendering to what seemed to be the inevitable. "I can only give you my side of the story,'' she cautioned. "Your father's version is probably very different.''

"Just tell me what you can tell me.''

And so Phoebe did. Hesitantly at first, then with increasing fluency, she offered her account of the past month. Lauralee listened silently, occasionally wrinkling her brow or nibbling on her lower lip.

"—and so I left,'' Phoebe finally concluded. "And I haven't seen your father since.''

The teenager sighed heavily. "I didn't know all that stuff about your fiancé, Phoebe. Or about your parents. I mean, I knew your mama and daddy were dead because you said so the first time we met, but I didn't realize . . .''

"I don't talk about it very much.''

Lauralee tilted her head to one side, her blue eyes thoughtful. "Maybe you should.''

It was not a new notion. "Maybe you're right.''

There was a break in the conversation then. Phoebe sat very still. She felt fragile and empty, like a blown eggshell. Lauralee shifted in her chair several times, looking around the office. Finally her gaze settled on the newspaper lying open on Phoebe's desk.

"Are you goin' to move?'' she asked unhappily, gesturing toward the classified ads.

"I think it'd be best all around if I did."

"Can we still be friends?"

"I'd like that very much," Phoebe responded honestly. "But your father might not approve."

Lauralee got to her feet. She cocked her chin, her delicate features taking on a determined cast. "I'll handle Daddy."

Phoebe stood up, too, alarmed by the teenager's attitude. While she clung to the hope that Jackson might someday understand why she'd acted as she had, she knew he'd never forgive her if she caused a schism with his daughter. "I don't want to be a source of trouble between you two, Lauralee."

"Don't worry, Phoebe," Lauralee said firmly. She looked around the office once again, then fluffed her curls. "Well, uh, thanks for seein' me."

"I'm glad you came." Phoebe moved out from behind her desk. "I'm sorry I avoided you the past two days. It's just been...difficult...to know what to say."

"That's okay." To Phoebe's surprise, Lauralee closed the distance between them and gave her a quick hug. Then the teenager turned and crossed to the door of the office. She had it halfway open when she suddenly pivoted back. "Phoebe?"

"Yes, Lauralee?"

"Did you mean what you said, about lovin' Daddy?"

Phoebe's throat went dry. She swallowed hard, several times, then passed her tongue over her lips. "Yes," she managed to respond.

"And what you said about bein' so afraid of losin' him?"

This time, Phoebe nodded. She didn't trust her voice.

"Well, didn't you make what you were afraid of happen?" Lauralee asked slowly. She seemed to be puzzling the question out as she went along. "I mean, isn't breakin' up with Daddy and never seein' him again pretty much the same as losin' him?"

Click.
Scratch-scratch. Scratch-scratch.

Jackson stiffened as he watched his daughter stab the yolk of her fried egg with her fork then drag the tines back and forth across her plate.

Click.

Scratch-scratch. Scratch-scratch.

Lauralee repeated the ritual with grim precision. Jackson felt his nerves tighten toward the snapping point.

Click.

Scratch-scra—

"Lauralee?"

His daughter froze, then lifted her head. There were shadowy smudges beneath her blue eyes. "What?"

"I think you've about killed that egg."

Lauralee lowered her gaze, then set down the fork. A moment later, she shoved the plate away.

Jackson frowned. "Are you all right?"

A shrug.

"Sugar—"

Lauralee's head came up again. Her expression was defiant. "I went to talk to Phoebe yesterday. At her office. While you were at work."

There was a long pause.

"I see," Jackson finally responded, fighting to keep his voice neutral.

"Well, *you* wouldn't tell me what happened!"

"But...she...would." He couldn't say Phoebe's name aloud. Not yet. It hurt too much.

"She explained her side." Lauralee blinked several times. When she resumed speaking her voice was trembling. "Phoebe l-loves you a lot, Daddy."

Jackson felt his guts twist. "Not enough," he countered bitterly.

Lauralee got up from the breakfast table and crossed to the refrigerator. Jackson heard her yank the door open, rummage around inside for several moments, then slam the door shut once again. He drank a mouthful of lukewarm coffee from the mug sitting at his right elbow.

Damn her, he thought. *Damn her!*

"D-Daddy?"

Something in Lauralee's tone prompted Jackson to turn around and look at his daughter. "What is it?"

Lauralee said nothing. She simply stood there, clenching and unclenching her hands, her throat working convulsively.

"Lauralee?"

"Do you believe that if somebody loves you the right amount, they won't be scared about what you do?"

The desperate-sounding question caught Jackson completely off guard. "I...I don't understand," he said after a few moments.

Lauralee took a step forward. She was trembling and her eyes were awash in tears. "I love you more than anythin', Daddy," she told him. "But I'm *scared* of your job. Of somethin' happenin' to you. Every day when you go to w-work, there's this l-little voice in me that keeps askin' 'What if...what if he doesn't come home this time?' And on Monday, when we w-went to see Fridge in the h-hospital? All I could think was it m-might have been you in that b-bed with all those t-t-tubes...."

"Oh, sugar." Jackson opened his arms. His daughter stumbled across the floor to him and collapsed into his lap, burrowing her head against his chest and sobbing. He cuddled her the way he'd done when she was a little girl. "Oh, sugar. Shh. Shh. It's okay, Lauralee. It's okay."

"I'm s-s-sorry, Daddy."

"There's no need for you to be sorry." He stroked his daughter's short, silky hair with shaking fingers, trying to contend with a powerful sense of shame. "Baby, I had no idea you felt this way."

"I wasn't—" a strangled hiccup "—s'posed to say anythin'."

His hand stilled. "What?"

"I w-wasn't s'posed—"

Jackson hooked a thumb beneath Lauralee's chin and tilted her face up toward his. "Who told you you weren't supposed to say anything about being afraid?"

She blinked, tears streaming down her cheeks. He knew the answer before she gave it. "Grammy M-Miller."

Jackson experienced a terrible flash of rage followed by something very close to pity. "My mother?"

Lauralee nodded tentatively, then gave another hiccupy sob.

"When was this, sugar?"

His daughter knuckled at her cheeks, sniffling. "'Member about four years ago, when you g-got shot?"

"Uh-huh."

"Well, afterward, when you went back to work, I started havin' n-nightmares about awful things happenin' to you. Grammy was stayin' over then, baby-sittin' me. I...I t-told her about my nightmares and said I was goin' to tell you. But she said I shouldn't because it would only make your j-job harder than it already was. She said bein' brave was part of the M-Miller Family tradition."

"Oh, Lauralee." Jackson hugged his only child. "Oh, baby."

"She said—" a long, drawn-out snuffle "—she'd explained everythin' to mama when you decided to join the department and that mama would've...would've explained it to m-me if she hadn't d-died."

Jackson rocked Lauralee gently for nearly a minute, silently berating himself for having been a blind and selfish fool. The Miller Family tradition of bravery— God! The Miller Family tradition of denial was more like it.

Phoebe had sensed the potentially destructive emotional dynamics that shaped his life without fully comprehending their source. *That's* why she'd asked so many questions about his marriage and his parents'. She'd also had the courage to tell him how she truly felt. And for that—dear Lord, for that he'd denounced her as a coward!

Jackson drew a deep breath. No more, he vowed. "Lauralee?"

His daughter's head came up. "W-what?"

"Do you want me to quit the department?"

Lauralee looked utterly shocked. "Quit? No, D-Daddy. Oh, no! I'm *proud* of you bein' a firefighter. What you d-do is important. Y-you—you *saved* Fridge's life! I just...I just wanted you to know that s-sometimes, well, n-not every-body's as fearless as you are."

"Oh, sugar." Jackson shook his head. Leaning forward, he picked up a paper napkin from the kitchen table and used it to blot his daughter's damp cheeks. "I'm a lot of things, but fearless isn't one of them. I'm as scared as the next man. Maybe *more* scared."

"You never show it." Lauralee took the napkin from her father, blew her nose, then dropped the sodden wad of paper onto the table.

"That's a kind of cowardice, too," Jackson responded, his throat tight. "Hiding feelings, instead of handling them."

Lauralee took a few moments to absorb this, her eyes flicking back and forth, back and forth. Finally she asked, "Do you hate Phoebe, Daddy?"

The question cut like a knife. Jackson tried not to flinch from the pain. "Is that what she thinks?"

"I'm not sure."

"I was angry with her. And with myself, probably, although I didn't realize it. But, no. I don't hate Phoebe. What I feel for her is about as far from hate as you can get."

Lauralee sighed and leaned against his chest. "When I was little, I believed that no matter how bad things were, you could always make them turn out right."

Jackson blinked against the sudden sting of tears. "You've wised up since then, huh?"

A second sigh. "I still believe you can *try*, Daddy."

Jackson dropped a kiss on the curly haired crown of his daughter's head. "So do I, sugar," he whispered. "So do I."

Phoebe slapped shut the file she'd been attempting to study for the past twenty minutes. Pulling off her horn-rimmed reading glasses, she tossed them onto her desk and began to massage the bridge of her nose.

She was in rocky shape and she knew it. What's more, her hospital colleagues obviously knew it, too. She'd lost count of the number of people who'd recently inquired if she was

"okay." At least a half dozen of them had indicated—wit
varying degrees of tact—that if she needed someone to tal
to, they were more than willing to listen.

Sometime during the past week or so, she'd been full
accepted into the staff hierarchy. She was no longer bein
treated as an outsider. She'd become part of the team. It wa
ironic, really. Her professional life was coming together a
the same time her personal life was falling to pieces. S
much for achieving a balanced existence!

She had to do something . . . and she had to do it soo
She'd be no good to anyone—not herself, not her pa
tients—if she continued the way she'd been.

Phoebe slumped into her chair and closed her eyes. Th
words Lauralee Miller had said to her two days earlier ecl
oed through her brain.

"Didn't you make what you were afraid of happen?" th
teenager had asked. *"I mean, isn't breakin' up with Dada
and never seein' him again pretty much the same as losir
him?"*

Phoebe inhaled shakily, finally acknowledging the trutl
Lauralee was right. She'd inflicted this loss on herself. She'
heeded the counsel of her fears and ignored her other fee
ings.

What did she want for herself? Some kind of hermet
cally sealed existence in which she could be totally isolate
from pain? Did she truly aspire to spend the rest of her yea
holding back, holding off, holding herself aloof? What kir
of psychiatrist would she be if she did that? What kind (
human being?

Phoebe opened her eyes. She loved Jackson Stuart Mi
ler. She loved him with every fiber of her being. She couldn
—*wouldn't*— let her fear of what might happen destroy tha
truth!

There weren't any promises of happily-ever-afters in tl
real world. Living—loving—didn't come with money-bac
guarantees. But unless a person were willing to take a risk.

Phoebe straightened in her chair. She picked up the tel
phone and punched in the seven digits she'd read in a cla
sified ad nearly eleven weeks earlier.

One ring.

Two rings.

Three—

A *click* of connection.

"Hello?" Phoebe said instantly.

A faint hiss warned her what she'd hear next.

"Hi," Jackson's recorded voice said. "This is 555-4963.
orry we can't answer the phone right now. Please leave
our name, number and a message. We'll get back to you as
oon as we can."

Beep.

"Jackson, this is Phoebe," Phoebe said, struggling to
eep her voice steady. "I need to talk to you. I'm still at the
ospital right now. I'm going to stop by and see Fridge when
get done with work. I should be home by seven-thirty. I
ope you'll be there." She swallowed. "I . . . I l-love you,
ackson."

She was shaking when she dropped the receiver back into
s cradle. She was still shaking nearly a minute later when
e telephone shrilled. She snatched it up, her heart pound-
g, her breath coming in shallow little puffs.

"Hello?"

"Dr. Donovan?"

The voice on the other end of the line wasn't Jackson's.
hoebe forced herself to shove aside a bitter sense of dis-
ppointment. "Yes, this is Dr. Donovan."

"Dr. Donovan, this is Emergency Admitting. Is Chris-
opher Barnett a patient of yours?"

A chill skittered up Phoebe's spine. "I have a Christo-
her Barnett in one of my therapy groups," she responded,
nmediately picturing a skinny, sullen-eyed teenager who
ame to—but seldom participated in—her Friday after-
oon out-patient sessions for adolescent substance abusers.

"Well, we have a teenager by that name locked up in one
f the examination rooms down here. He's got a scalpel and
e's threatening to use it on himself. He keeps asking for
ou."

"Now, ma'am—"

"Officer, I am not a 'ma'am,'" Phoebe snapped at the

balding and burly security guard who was blocking her wa
"I am a *doctor.* A doctor with a patient who needs me."

"That patient has a scalpel, ma—uh, Doctor."

"He hasn't used it on anybody, has he?"

"Well, uh, no. But he's threatenin'—"

"To turn it on himself. Yes, I know. *That's* why I'm tel
ing you to let me into his examining room right now."

"I don't think—"

"No one's asking you to. Just allow me to do my job!"

The guard scowled for a moment, then stepped aside. "
anythin' happens—"

"Don't worry, I won't sue."

Christopher Barnett was huddled in the far corner of t
examining room. His head snapped up the instant Phoeb
opened the door. His right arm shot forward, a glitterir
scalpel blossoming from his white-knuckled fist.

"Hi, Chris," Phoebe said softly. "It's Dr. Donovan."

"Just you!" the teenager cried, trying to press himse
farther into the corner. "Nobody else!"

"That's right," Phoebe agreed, easing into the roon
"Just me. Nobody else." She let the door close behind he
"I hear you wanted to talk to me."

The boy's eyes shifted back and forth. His pupils we
unusually dilated. There was an unhealthy sheen of sweat o
the pimple-pocked skin of his forehead and cheeks. '
was... I was gonna call the Hotline," he said, slurring tl
words a bit. "But I forgot the number."

"That happens, Chris."

He shuddered suddenly, drawing his knees up and h
arms inward. "Are you mad at me?"

"Because you forgot a telephone number? Of cour
not."

"Those people—those people out there—" The teenag
jerked his head toward the door.

"They're not mad at you, either."

"They were! They—they wanted to hurt me!"

"Is that why you thought you needed the scalpel?"

Chris glanced down at the object in his right hand the
back up at Phoebe. "I don't... I don't remember."

"That's okay, Chris," Phoebe quickly reassured him. "Do you remember what you wanted to talk to me about?"

The teenager blinked rapidly several times, another shudder running through him. After a few moments, he levered himself up into a standing position. "I...I took some p-pills. I said...I said I w-wouldn't, but I d-did."

"Pills?" Phoebe fought to keep her voice calm. "Do you know what kind of pills?"

Chris shook his head, swaying slightly. "White ones, maybe. Or blue. I don't—" He broke off, his face contorting. Tears began seeping from the corners of his eyes. "Are you mad at me, Dr. D-Donovan? *Are you?*"

"No, I'm not mad at you. How could I be? Yes, you took pills and that isn't good for you. But you were smart enough to come here for help, Chris. That *is* what you did—isn't it?"

"Y-yeah." He dragged the back of his left hand under his nose. "I think...think so."

"I *know* so, Chris." Phoebe paused, gauging the boy's condition, mentally matching his symptoms against various illegal substances. "Look, I'm going to come a little closer to you, all right?"

"Not too close!"

"No, not too close." She took one step forward. Then another. "Okay?"

"Okay."

"Great. Now, why don't you come a little closer to me?"

"I—"

"Just two steps, Chris. Please? That's it. First your right foot. Then your left foot. Terrific. Now, I'm going to put out my hand so you can give me the scalpel."

A vigorous head shake.

"You don't need it anymore, Chris. Nobody's mad at you. Everybody wants to help you. I'm not going to *take* the scalpel. I'm asking you to *give* it to me."

"You won't...you won't take it?"

"I won't take it." Phoebe extended her right hand, palm up. "Please, Chris. Give me the scalpel."

There was a moment's hesitation, then the teenager com
plied with her request. He gave her the scalpel, blade first
slicing her flesh open from the base of her index finger to the
top of her wrist.

The injury wasn't intentional. Phoebe would stake her
professional reputation on that. Indeed, the look of horror
on Chris's face when he realized what he'd done was truly
awful to see.

"I d-didn't m-mean—" he began shrilly, backing away
from her. "Dr. D-Donovan, I d-didn't— Oh, help! Some
body c-come in and *help!*"

"It's—it's all right, Chris," Phoebe said, clutching her
bleeding hand against her chest. It hurt. It hurt like hell. Her
head began to swim. Her vision blurred. She heard the door
to the examining room burst open.

"I'm sorry!" the teenager cried. "I'm sorry!"

Controlled chaos.

Choreographed confusion.

For the second time in her life, Dr. Phoebe Irene Dono
van keeled over in a dead faint.

Thirteen

_____

"Phoebe?"

Jackson's voice. She'd know it anywhere.

"Phoebe?"

His voice was so tender. And she could feel him touching
r. Gently. Oh, so gently.

It had to be a dream.

But if it was a dream, why did she hurt so much? Why
as her skull aching and her right hand throbbing? Weren't
eams supposed to be—

"Open your eyes for me, Phoebe."

Phoebe did as she'd been bidden. For a few seconds,
erything was blurred. Then the formless blobs shimmer-
g across her field of vision coalesced into the strong-
atured face of the man she loved. He was leaning over her
d he was *smiling*.

"Jackson," she whispered.

"Hey, darlin'," he greeted her, brushing his fingertips
ghtly against her cheek. "I thought *I* was supposed to be
e one with the dangerous job."

Phoebe gave a weak laugh, then winced against a sudd
hammer stroke of pain in her temples. "My...my head—'

"Easy," Jackson soothed. "You conked yourself on t
corner of the examining table when you passed out."

"When I—?" Memory returned in a sickening rush. S
started to sit up. "Chris—"

"No, you don't," Jackson said firmly, easing her ba
down. "The kid's doing all right. They pumped his sto:
ach. Whatever it was he took, he didn't take enough to
any permanent damage."

"Thank heavens." Phoebe ran her tongue over her li;
They felt dry and scaly.

"Here, darlin'."

Jackson brought a small plastic glass to her mouth. S
sipped. Ice water had never tasted so good. It trickled do
her throat like a liquid benediction.

When she'd drunk her fill, Jackson took the glass aw
and stroked her cheek once again. The look in his sl
colored eyes made her weak in a way that had nothing to
with the injuries she'd sustained in the emergency room.

"What...what are you doing here?" she asked, lifting
left hand and skimming the line of his jaw.

Jackson turned his face into her hand and kissed
palm. Then he took her left hand in his right and held
"Aside from being scared out of a good ten years of
life?"

"You were frightened for me?"

"Oh, Phoebe." He shook his head, his eyes cloudi:
"When I came into this room and saw you..."

"But *why* did you come to the hospital?"

Jackson gave her hand a gentle squeeze. "I came
cause I got your message."

All the air she had in her lungs left in a rush. "Oh," s
managed to say.

He smiled. The clouds in his eyes vanished. "I love yc
too, darlin'. I love you, and I want to marry you."

"You...you do?"

"More than anything in the world, Phoebe. But before you give me an answer, I have to tell you I'm not the same man I was when I proposed four days ago."

"You're not?"

"I hope you'll think I'm a better one. To begin with, I'm in line for a promotion. I'm also being reassigned. To the fire academy."

Ignoring the pain it caused, Phoebe shook her head. "No," she protested. "You don't—I don't want you to do this for me—"

He captured her face between his work-hardened palms. "It's not just for you, darlin'. It's for *us*. For our future together." His mouth curled into a tender smile. "And for Lauralee."

She searched his eyes and saw nothing but truth. "Are you sure?"

"The only thing I'm any surer of is my feelings for you."

"Oh, Jackson."

"Will you marry me, Phoebe? Please?"

"Yes! Oh, yes..."

Dr. Phoebe Irene Donovan and soon-to-be Captain Jackson Stuart Miller were married two weeks later. Because the best man, Fire Officer Ralph "Fridge" Randall, was on the mend but still confined to bed, the wedding took place in his hospital room.

The bride had two attendants. Keezia Carew performed her duties as matron-of-honor with characteristic elan and efficiency, yet she was obviously more interested in the best man than in anything else. Lauralee Miller made a lovely maid-of-honor, although her new stepmother suspected her dreamy-eyed radiance had something to do with the fact that a young man named Tommy John Purdy had finally summoned up the courage to do something more than listen on the end of a telephone line. How Lauralee's daddy would react to this development was something the bride decided to defer investigating until after the honeymoon.

The groom's mother was one of the few guests invited to the simple but joyous event. While Louisa Miller gave her apparently sincere blessing to the union and a very expensive strand of pearls to the bride, she did not offer—nor was she asked for—any advice about being the wife of a firefighter.

At the conclusion of the ceremony, the newlyweds kissed. Once at the urging of the minister. Once strictly for themselves.

Long before that second kiss ended, an ancient spark flared and gave birth to a flame that burned bright and pure.

The flame was true love and it was more powerful than any fear.

* * * * *

SILHOUETTE® *Desire*
MAN OF THE MONTH: 1993

**They're tough, they're sexy...
and they know how to get the
job done....
Caution: They're**

MEN AT WORK

Blue collar... white collar... these men are working overtime
to earn your love.

July:	Undercover agent Zeke Daniels in Annette Broadrick's ZEKE
August:	Aircraft executive Steven Ryker in Diana Palmer's NIGHT OF LOVE
September:	Entrepreneur Joshua Cameron in Ann Major's WILD HONEY
October:	Cowboy Jake Tallman in Cait London's THE SEDUCTION OF JAKE TALLMAN
November:	Rancher Tweed Brown in Lass Small's TWEED
December:	Engineer Mac McLachlan in BJ James's ANOTHER TIME, ANOTHER PLACE

Let these men make a direct deposit into your heart.
MEN AT WORK... only from Silhouette Desire!

ANN MAJOR
SOMETHING WILD

Take a walk on the *wild* side with Ann Major's sizzling stories featuring Honey, Midnight...and Innocence!

September 1993 WILD HONEY
Man of the Month
A clash of wills sets the stage for an electrifying romance for J. K. Cameron and Honey Wyatt.

November 1993 WILD MIDNIGHT
Heat Up Your Winter
A bittersweet reunion turns into a once-in-a-lifetime adventure for Lacy Douglas and Johnny Midnight.

February 1994 WILD INNOCENCE
Man of the Month
One man's return sets off a startling chain of events for Innocence Lescuer and Raven Wyatt.

Let your wilder side take over with this exciting series—only from Silhouette Desire!

Premiere

Silhouette Books has done it again!

Opening night in October has never been as exciting! Come watch as
the curtain rises and romance flourishes when the stars of tomorrow
make their debuts today!

Revel in Jodi O'Donnell's STILL SWEET ON HIM—
Silhouette Romance #969
...as Callie Farrell's renovation of the family homestead leads her
straight into the arms of teenage crush Drew Barnett!

Tingle with Carol Devine's BEAUTY AND THE BEASTMASTER—
Silhouette Desire #816
...as legal eagle Amanda Tarkington is carried off by wrestler
Bram Masterson!

Thrill to Elyn Day's A BED OF ROSES—
Silhouette Special Edition #846
...as Dana Whitaker's body and soul are healed by sexy physical
therapist Michael Gordon!

Believe when Kylie Brant's McLAIN'S LAW—
Silhouette Intimate Moments #528
...takes you into detective Connor McLain's life as he falls for
psychic—and suspect—Michele Easton!

Catch the classics of tomorrow—*premiering* today—
only from ❤ *Silhouette*

WOLFE WAITING
by Joan Hohl

This big, bad Wolfe never had to huff and puff and blow down *any* woman's door—scrumptiously sexy rookie officer Jake Wolfe was just too tempting and tasty to leave outside in the cold! But then he got hungry for answers from the suspicious lady who wouldn't let him two feet near her. What was a big, bad Wolfe to do?

Huff and puff *your* way to your favorite retail outlet before *Wolfe Waiting*—Book One of Joan Hohl's sexy BIG, BAD WOLFE series—is all gobbled up! Only from Silhouette Desire in September....

SDBBW1

**Silhouette Books
is proud to present
our best authors,
their best books...
and the best in
your reading pleasure!**

Throughout 1993, look for exciting
books by these top names in
contemporary romance:

DIANA PALMER—
Fire and Ice in June

ELIZABETH LOWELL—
Fever in July

CATHERINE COULTER—
Afterglow in August

LINDA HOWARD—
Come Lie With Me in September

When it comes to passion,
we wrote the book.

BOBT2

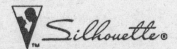